Maryalise

and the Singing Flowers

Maryalise

and the Singing Flowers

Book One of the Maryalise Trilogy

Rose Owens

Cover Art by Keliana Tayler

http://www.KelianaRTayler.com

ISBN- 9781723384486

To Jerry

And my family

Because they love and believe in me.

Table of Contents

The Dark Dragon

The dark dragon swooped closer. Each stroke of its powerful wings sent furious winds howling towards her. Lightning slashed. The blue vanished and the sky rapidly became storm dark. Thunder crashed. The furious wind shrieked as it beat against the window. An ominous dark shape advanced towards her. *It's only a storm cloud*, Mary Alice thought. *It isn't really a dragon. It isn't.* Her fingers clenched and unclenched as she stared out the living room window. *Am I imagining it? Aunt Janet says I imagine too much.* Fear clutched her heart and would not let go. *It isn't my imagination. It isn't.*

A jagged flash of light revealed the dark silhouette of a woman standing on the dragon's back. Long slender fingers reached out. *I'm safe*, Mary Alice told herself. *She can't get me.* But she felt as if those fingers might grab her and hold her captive.

Although she feared what was outside, she felt compelled to move closer to the window. She stood at the side, peering around the curtain. The darkness in the garden oozed through the window, and black despair slithered into her heart. She lifted her eyes to the threatening sky. Clouds covered the sun and shadowed the garden. The raging wind beat against the window, and she backed away. The dragon whirled and vanished into the darkness. Had she imagined the woman and the dragon?

The dark outside echoed the darkness in her heart. *Who am I? They call me Mary Alice, but that doesn't feel right. Where are my parents? And why can't I remember them*? Her thoughts were all jumbled and mixed up. *Oh, why can't I remember?*

It seemed that the howling wind wanted inside. Its savage roar echoed in her ears. She covered them with her hands. In spite of the noise of the wind, she heard soft music. So she lowered her hands and listened intently. The music was here in this room. She turned around and saw a Victorian lamp on the small table beside the sofa. The music was coming from it.

She walked across the room and looked at the lamp. The bottom of it was like a vase with gold trim. The shiny fabric of the lampshade was covered with vines and pink flowers. Crystal prisms were hanging from little hooks all around the bottom of the shade. They swung gently back and forth. *The crystals are making the music, and it sounds like magic music*. She reached out and lifted one from its little hook. Her heart didn't beat quite so fast now.

She cradled the crystal in her hands, and her thoughts returned to the name that didn't seem to be hers. *Mary Alice is such a plain name,* she thought, *a child's name. I'm not a child. I'm twelve. I'd rather be named Maryalise.* A calm, peaceful feeling wrapped itself around her. She smiled. *From now on I will think of myself as Maryalise. It will be my secret name.*

The soft music from the crystals on the lampshade surrounded her. Holding her crystal up, she placed it between herself and the angry storm. She chanted:

Magic in this crystal. Magic in me.
Magic in this crystal. Magic in me.
Send sunshine gleaming, sunshine beaming.
Send a ray of sunshine through this storm.

A ray of sunshine pierced the darkness and flew to the crystal in her hand. More light bounced off the lamp's swinging crystals, and dancing rainbows filled the room. *Did I really do that?* It felt like magic. Lightness and joy surrounded her, inviting her to dance. She rose to her toes, and her slender body swayed back and forth. Her feet began to move. Her honey brown hair flowed as she twirled. She felt as if magic gathered around her. *I'm as light as a fairy*. Her feet abruptly stopped moving. *Why did I think that? Fairies are pretend, aren't they*? She shrugged slightly and held the crystal higher and danced from rainbow to rainbow, gathering their strength and magic into herself.

"Mary Alice! Mary Alice! Whatever are you doing?"

She stopped. The feeling of being Maryalise was gone. She was Mary Alice, and she was in trouble—again! She looked into Aunt Janet's angry eyes. Her aunt was tall and bony. She had gray hair that was confined in a tight bun. Not a hair dared to escape. *Which one of Aunt Janet's rules did I forget this time*? Mary Alice wondered.

She looked around. Darkness shadowed the room once more. The rainbows and the music were gone and the wind continued its angry howl. She quickly lowered her hand and hid the crystal behind her back.

"Just what did you think you were doing?" demanded Aunt Janet. The frown wrinkles between her eyebrows matched the stern set of her mouth.

Mary Alice hung her head. Her eyes slipped downward, past the precise collar on Aunt Janet's dress and she looked at each of the tiny buttons marching down the front of it. Her eyes settled on her aunt's sensible shoes. *Dancing,* Mary Alice thought.

Someone else's thought drifted across the room and slipped into Mary Alice's mind. *How beautiful she is when she dances. How magical!*

She wondered where that thought had come from. *From Aunt Janet? I know that I didn't think it.* The thought floated in the air between them. In the stunned silence, she looked up and saw a gentleness in her aunt's eyes that she had not seen before. For just a moment Mary Alice became Maryalise and her mind reached out to Aunt Janet's. *Why can I. . .*

A startled expression flickered in her aunt's eyes and then vanished. Being Maryalise vanished too.

What happened? wondered Mary Alice. *Aunt Janet's eyes are angry again. I heard her thoughts. Did I imagine that?*

Her aunt crossed her arms, leaned forward and repeated her question. "Just what did you think you were doing?"

Mary Alice hung her head. Her fingers clasped the crystal tighter and she whispered, "Dancing."

Tears blurred her vision. She blinked her eyes quickly to keep them from escaping. *Aunt Janet doesn't understand. I don't think she likes me.* She remembered how often this aunt criticized her. *Does she really want me here?*

Aunt Janet's lips snapped shut, making an angry straight line across her face. She glared at her niece. Mary Alice avoided looking directly at her aunt and cautiously slipped the crystal into the pocket of her dress.

She saw Aunt Lillian standing in the hall. Her cheerful smile was missing. Aunt Janet had that hard, bony look, but Aunt Lillian was shorter and softer. She had silver streaks in her mousey brown hair. Although her hair was pulled back into a soft bun, wisps of silver always escaped and curled around her face. Aunt Lillian walked across the room and patted Mary Alice on the shoulder. Her eyes twinkled. "Don't worry," she said. "Janet will calm down. Go find something else to do." Then she leaned over and whispered in Mary Alice's ear. "We used to play in the attic on stormy days."

Aunt Lillian treats me like a child—but it makes her happy, thought Mary Alice. She continued thinking about her aunts as she slowly climbed the stairs to the second floor. They were old. She could believe that Aunt Lillian was once a little girl who played in the attic, but it was hard to think that Aunt Janet had ever been a child. She tucked her thoughts away to think about later.

When she reached the door at the end of the hall, she opened it and began to climb the steep set of stairs that led up to the attic door. *Play? I'm twelve—not a child to be sent to play in the attic.* But she had nowhere else to go. She shook her head and sighed. *I may as well go to the attic.*

The Attic

It's dark in here. Mary Alice turned on the light. The only source of light was a bare bulb hanging in the center of the room. There were cobwebs in the corners and dust covered everything. It was clear that no one had been up here recently.

She slowly walked past three little chairs and a small table tucked beneath the sloping ceiling. The shabby rocking horse had peeling paint and a cracked smile on its face. A cardboard box held rolls of wallpaper. There were stacks of old books, boxes of old clothes, blankets, and dishes—all the things that no one really wanted anymore but were too good to throw away. They all had been stored in the attic.

Junk, she thought. *There's nothing here but junk.* She wandered over to the small window on the far side of the room. The dust on the window was so thick that she couldn't see through it. She lifted her hand and smeared a hole in the dust. Then she wiped her grimy hand on the skirt of her dress.

Mary Alice peered through the window. *Is that woman still out there? On the dragon?* She had no way of knowing. *The storm is still out there. Will it destroy Aunt Lillian's flowers?* She tilted her head to one side as she continued thinking. *And what about the willow tree? Is it safe?*

On the far side of the garden, the stream widened to form a small pool. An old willow tree stood sentinel, its branches sweeping down to the ground. There was a sheltered place under its branches. A circle of white stones, placed side by side, formed a circle around the tree. They always felt warm to her touch even though they were in the shade. This secret place was her refuge from Aunt Janet's expectations. Fear and hope twisted inside her as she looked at the storm in the garden. *Is my secret place safe?* She needed it to be safe.

She leaned her head against the cool glass and felt the storm beating outside. *I won't think about that right now. I can't. I have to think of something else.* She reached into her pocket and felt the crystal teardrop. Bringing it out, she held it aloft. *Would it really bring the sunshine?*

I will be Maryalise, she decided. She felt something change. She examined her hands and feet. She touched her face. It was very mysterious. Although her size and outward appearance had not changed, she felt different inside. She felt magical. *I'm Maryalise, and I have magic. I will finish the dance.* The song from the crystals entered her mind and heart. Swaying back and forth, she began her dance. Back and forth and around the room she flew. She paused by the window. Holding the crystal aloft, she whispered:

> Magic, I call the magic of the rainbow.
> Magic, magic, I call the magic of the sunbeams.
> Send your rays through this darkness.
> Bring your light to me.

The clouds parted. A ray of sunlight danced across the forbidding sky and through the window. It darted through the crystal and a rainbow appeared in the room. Mary Alice smiled. She waved the crystal back and forth and watched the rainbow dance around the room. It stopped above a pile of old blankets in the far corner of the room. Maryalise waved the crystal but the rainbow didn't move. She lowered the crystal, but the rainbow was still there. *It's magic. It has to be.* She stared down at the crystal. Even though the sun couldn't reach it, a spark of light still radiated from it. *There is magic in this crystal.*

The rainbow arched above the blankets and tiny sparkles drifted down. *It wants me to move the blankets.* She hurried across the room and pushed the blankets aside and saw a small chest. Maryalise lifted it from the pile of boxes and examined it. It had a curved top and brass trim. *It's just like the one I found under the willow tree.* She remembered that the other chest had been locked. *I wish I had been able to open it.* She cradled this one in her arms and smiled. It was identical to the one in her secret place, except this one had an initial "A" carved on the bottom instead of a "D." The lid of this one wouldn't open either. She rubbed her hand across the front of the chest, and her fingers found the invisible keyhole that her eyes couldn't see. *I think it's a magic chest. Will a magic spell open it?*

"Abracadabra. Open." The chest did not open.

"Hocus Pocus." Nothing happened.

"Open Sesame." It still would not open and she could not think of any more magic words to try.

She shook the chest. "I wish you would open." The chest remained closed. Touching the invisible lock once more, she said, "I wish I had the key." A small golden key appeared in her hand. Her eyes opened wide and she took a quick breath. "Oh!" *Where did that come from?* She fingered the key and the length of soft ribbon threaded through the hole at the top. She looked at the chest again. The keyhole was now visible.

Holding her breath, she carefully inserted the key into the lock and twisted it. There was a small click and the key vanished. Something dropped around her neck and a small object bumped against her body. She reached up and touched it with her hand. Although she could feel the key and the ribbon around her neck, she could not see it. *It's magic. My magic key.* She turned her attention back to the chest. *What will I find inside this chest—jewels? Magic objects?* She lifted the lid.

"Empty? The chest is empty!" she said. *But why? Why would someone bother to lock an empty chest with a magic lock*? She felt like crying. There was nothing in it! *But there has to be something inside. There just has to be!*

She looked again. Nothing. She put her hand inside the chest and felt carefully all around the bottom. Her fingers felt the edge of something that was wedged into the bottom of the chest. It felt small and flat. Carrying the chest to the center of the room, she set it down beneath the light bulb, knelt down, and looked inside.

Slipping her fingers under the edge of the object, she lifted it out of the chest. Folded pages were fastened together with an uneven stitch. *Someone made this notebook*, she thought. *Who does it belong to? What's in it?* She settled herself on the floor, opened the notebook and began to read.

This is my diary. It is a secret diary. Magic protects it. No mortal will be able to find it. No mortal will be able to read it.

If that's true, then why can I read this? I'm a mortal. Maybe being Maryalise makes a difference. She smiled and turned the page.

My name is Annie. This is the record of the magical adventures of three sisters—Annie and Flora and Denelia. We are magic. Each of us has a special magic. Together our magic is powerful. This is how we invoke our magic. First, we go to our secret place at the edge of the crystal stream. After making sure that no one sees us, one by one we part the willow branches and slip inside.

Maryalise stopped reading and closed her eyes. She thought of the old willow tree with the branches that arched upward and then hung down to touch the ground. A thrill of excitement swirled around her. *My secret place was their secret place.* Her excitement grew as she continued reading.

After entering our secret place, we inspect the magic circle and make sure that each stone is protecting its place. It is vital that the circle be complete.

Is that why the stones feel warm? Maryalise closed her eyes and remembered the circle of stones. *They protect that place under the willow tree?* Now she was anxious to learn more. She opened her eyes and continued reading.

We sit down in a circle—Flora, Denelia, and I. We make a circle of unity as we reach out and grasp hands. When the circle is complete, we can feel the magic move around the circle. We have magic—powerful magic. The magic grows stronger as we chant our secret names. No one knows our magic names except we three. I am . . .

Reaching the end of the page, Maryalise quickly turned it to find out what their magic names were.

But there was nothing! *What happened? I want to know their magical names.* She concentrated very hard and stared intently at the page, but it still was blank. The next pages were also blank. *They are all empty. Maybe two pages are stuck together.* She examined the pages carefully. They were not.

Turning to the front of the notebook, she read everything again and turned the page once more. It was still blank. A careful examination of the notebook revealed some ragged edges in the center where pages had been torn out. *Who ripped them out? What was written there?*

She looked in the chest. It was empty. The missing pages were not there. She looked under the chest. No pages there. She ran to the corner where the chest had been hidden. She looked behind the boxes and dug through the boxes. She could not find the missing pages.

"They have to be somewhere," she said. Returning to the middle of the room, she sat down and looked at the small notebook once more. Her finger traced the ragged edges where the pages had once been and she felt a tingle. "I think there is magic here," she muttered. "Magic protects this." She sat in silence and thought about magic. *I think. . . maybe I have magic. I'm going to try to bring the pages back.* She rose to her feet and began to dance. She lifted her arms toward the bare lightbulb above her head and coaxed its light down to the pages below. Music guided her steps, surrounding her with magic. She danced around the notebook and chanted:

Magic, I am magic.
I have powerful magic.
Restore all as it was before.
Bring back that which was lost.
By the magic in me, I command,
Missing words you must return,
Must be as you were before.

She twirled and tiny snowflakes appeared, swirling around her and settling one by one on the open notebook. She hesitated, stopped dancing, and lowered her arms. The snowflakes were actually small, torn pieces of paper. Tipping her head down, she watched one word after another appear on the page. It was as if each word was being dropped by an invisible hand.

Who am I? she wondered once again. *Why did I know a magic spell?*

"Mary Alice." Aunt Lillian's voice echoed up the stairs, intruding into her thoughts. "Mary Alice? It's time to eat."

"It's always time for something," Maryalise muttered under her breath as she became Mary Alice again. "Just when things get interesting, it's time for something else."

"I'm coming, Aunt Lillian," she called. "I'll be there in just a minute." She picked the notebook up and carefully closed it before returning it to the chest. There was a soft click as she closed the lid. Becoming Maryalise once again, she whispered the words of a spell to keep the notebook safe.

Magic, oh magic, I summon thee,
Hide the chest from all but me.
Notebook of Annie's,
Be safe in this chest.
Let no one find you.
Keep safe and wait for me.
By magic, this I command thee.

She placed the chest back in its corner and piled the blankets on top of it again. She looked back longingly one last time as she started toward the stairs. Now she was Mary Alice once more.

After she entered the kitchen, she sat down at the table without speaking. There were important things to think about, and she hardly noticed what she was eating.

"Who was Annie? When did Annie live here?" When she saw her aunts' faces, she realized that she had spoken out loud.

Aunt Lillian sat motionless with her spoon suspended halfway to her mouth.

Aunt Janet looked angry. She snapped, "There is no Annie. She's no one at all!"

I'm sure she was somebody, Mary Alice thought. *After all, I found her notebook.*

Aunt Lillian leaned forward and smiled. It was a dreamy smile as if—as if she were remembering something or someone. She said, "Annie was. . ."

Aunt Janet glared across the table at her sister.

Aunt Lillian shifted back in her chair. Her smile faded and she asked, "What made you imagine Annie?"

Mary Alice didn't say anything. *I don't think that was what Aunt Lillian started to say. And how can I explain about the attic and the chest and the notebook with Aunt Janet glaring at me like that? I wish I knew what Aunt Lillian was going to say.* Mary Alice wished she hadn't spoken. She wished—she didn't know what she wished. She just wanted to escape Aunt Janet's angry eyes. She ducked her head and concentrated on eating.

The Garden

The storm continued to rage during dinner and on into the evening. When Mary Alice went upstairs to go to bed, she stood at her bedroom window looking out into the darkness. *I still can't see the garden. Are the flowers safe? There's nothing except blackness out there*. She leaned her head against the window, feeling troubled. *I'm not scared—not exactly. But something about this storm makes me nervous*.

She heard footsteps behind her. Someone's arms circled around her and drew her close. Tipping her head back, she looked up. *Aunt Janet? I thought it would be Aunt Lillian.*

Her aunt smiled reassuringly. "It's all right Mary Alice. You are safe here inside the house. I won't let anything harm you." Aunt Janet was smiling.

The gesture and words were unlike the Aunt Janet that Mary Alice had learned to expect. However, at that moment she felt safe and protected. After her aunt left the room, Mary Alice slipped into bed, pulled up the covers and smiled. She had liked that smile. *Maybe Aunt Janet does love me, after all. Even if I do forget her rules.* She closed her eyes.

It was the silence that woke her early the next morning. It was still dark. There was no sound inside the house. She lay in bed and thought. *How quiet it is. Maybe everyone else is sleeping*. It was cozy in her bed. She watched as the darkness slipped away and rosy pink light peeked through her window. A ray of sunshine came dancing across the room to warm her face. Somewhere in the garden a bird began caroling its morning song.

She slipped from beneath the covers and hurried to the window. There were splashes of pink and lavender spreading across the sky. However, she could see threatening blackness in the distance across the horizon. The dark storm clouds rolled toward the garden. *The storm's coming again.* But there was something strange about those clouds. This time they stopped at the edge of the garden, and they didn't come any closer. *What is stopping those clouds? It's a storm waiting to happen, but something won't let it.*

In the garden down below, sunshine was creeping across the devastation. The rainbow of blossoms was no more. The daisies lay flat upon the ground, and the pansies were hidden beneath piles of wet leaves and mud. All of the flowers were bent and broken.

Mary Alice opened the window and listened. Sometimes she could hear a soft melody in the garden—as if the flowers were singing. The flowers were not singing this morning. She could see that a few dandelions stood proudly erect, their cheerful blossoms reaching up to catch the rays of sunshine. She looked up into the sky above the garden again. Seeing the morning star winking at her, she chanted:

Oh Morning Star, hear my plea.
Send sunshine down.
Banish clouds.
Leave only sunshine for me.

It's a little brighter now, she thought. The black clouds seemed farther away. She pulled on her light blue dress. She touched the daisies embroidered on the skirt. *Aunt Lillian made this for me*. The warmth of Aunt Lillian's love seemed to reach out and enfold her, like a hug. *Like magic.* Not bothering with stockings, she slipped on her shoes and tiptoed down the stairs, carefully avoiding the squeaky step.

She stood on the porch and stared at the destruction before her. She wanted to go to her secret place under the willow tree, but she had not yet done her morning chores. She knew if she asked to go out into the garden now, Aunt Janet would probably say no. She looked over her shoulder. Her aunt wasn't anywhere in sight. *So I won't ask*, she decided. *I can be back before she even knows I'm awake.* Looking at all the mud, she thought about those rules once more. *She'll be mad if I get my shoes muddy. So I'll go barefoot.* After her shoes were hidden behind a large flower pot, she ran down the steps and into the garden.

She was almost at the willow tree when she heard someone speaking. She stopped, crouched low, and waited. There was no indication that whoever was speaking had either seen or heard her. She cautiously moved forward. Aunt Janet was wandering through the garden, stopping occasionally to stare at crushed blossoms. "Oh dear. Oh my. This should not have happened. I should never have let it happen. It must not happen again."

Does Aunt Janet think she could stop a storm? wondered Mary Alice. After her aunt had moved on down the path, she continued her own journey. She cautiously slipped around the edge of the garden, keeping behind the bushes, looking to make sure no one could see her before she dashed across the bare places.

Eventually, she reached the willow tree. She became Maryalise as she parted the branches. She knelt down on the muddy ground and touched one of the white stones. It felt warm to her touch. *I can feel the magic here*, she thought as she crawled over the stones. A few drops of water fell on her head, but the inside of her secret place was mostly dry. *It's safe! I'm glad the storm didn't get inside*. She examined the magic circle. It was complete. Everything was exactly the same as before.

I will be Maryalise, she told herself. She sat cross-legged and tried to think about what she should do. The storm had destroyed the garden. She sat very still and searched within herself for the right spell to heal the garden. The words didn't come. *I need help. I wish I had someone to talk to—like those three girls.*

When she thought of them, she remembered that this was their secret place. She needed a calling spell. No, that wasn't the right word for it. Then she remembered that Aunt Janet would often say, "Lillian, will you summon Mary Alice for supper?" *That's it. I need a summoning spell.*

Now it was as if she heard a voice whisper in her mind and give her words to say. She closed her eyes, placed her hands in her lap and chanted the words:

I summon you, summon you,
Call you here from far away.
Annie, Flora, Denelia,
I need you here today.

She held out her hands—palms upward—and felt magic. Opening her eyes, she saw a misty sphere hovering beside her. It became larger and formed itself into the shape of a girl who sat down and gently placed her left hand upon Maryalise's right hand. There was a tingle of magic.

Maryalise held her breath as she saw another misty sphere appear and form itself into the shape of another girl who was identical to the first one. This girl moved around the circle of magic stones, lightly touching each one before sitting down and clasping the hand of the first girl. The tingle of magic grew stronger.

There was still an empty place in the circle. A third sphere appeared. It dipped and danced around Maryalise and the two indistinct girls. Then the sphere formed itself into the shape of a third girl who looked like the first two. Sitting down, she reached out with one hand to clasp the hand of the second girl. She laid her other hand on the palm of Maryalise's left hand. Each girl was faint, shadowy—like a spirit. No words were voiced aloud, but Maryalise heard them think in unison, *The circle of unity is complete.*

The magic spiraled around the circle, gaining strength and becoming more powerful. Now she could see the girls more clearly and could identify their features. Each girl had honey brown hair. *They have freckles—just like me. They seem to be about my age.*

They did not speak out loud, but words formed in her mind. *We give you power—magic power. Remember who you are. Remember what you are. You can heal the garden. You will win.* The girls smiled at her.

Win what? Maryalise thought. *Remember what? I've already tried to remember.* She closed her eyes and tried once more to remember anything about her past. It seemed as if there was an elusive memory floating near her, but it wasn't clear. Suddenly her hands were empty. She opened her eyes. She was alone in the shelter of the willow tree. The three girls were gone. But the magic feeling remained. I'm not pretending, she told herself. *I do have magic.I do.*

She wished the three girls had stayed. *At least I know they are real. I summoned them and they came. But who is who?* She felt she should know them. Reaching back for a memory once more, she waited. Nothing came. She couldn't find a memory of them, and she couldn't find a memory of her past self. *I can't remember anyone but my two aunts. Why?*

She wrinkled her forehead as she considered this puzzle. *I must have a mother and a father. Everyone does. But where are they? And why did they leave me here?* There was a tightness squeezing her—as if someone was pinching her heart. *Who am I?*

Maybe it was time for a new spell—a remembering spell. Closing her eyes, she tried to think of rhyming words. She finally decided on the words for her spell, but she wasn't sure if it was a good one because she couldn't think of any rhyming words. Spells were better with rhyming words. She tipped her head to the side and wondered, *How do I know that?* Since she had no answer to that question, she took a deep breath, closed her eyes and chanted:

Remember, oh remember.
Oh, rays of sunshine,
Sparkling rainbows,
Morning Star.
Help me, please.
Help me remember
The things that I have forgotten

.

No memories came. *There is a wall blocking my memories, and I have banged into it.* She rested her elbows on her knees and tucked her chin into her hands. She shook her head back and forth. It wasn't fair. She gritted her teeth, concentrated harder and examined that invisible wall. It was high and wide and hard. She could not see it, but it was there. And it blocked her memories. *I am here and my memories are over there.*

Every question she thought about her parents or her childhood hit that wall and bounced back at her. Her aunts were on this side with her. *Who is on the other side? The wall won't let me see.* She scrunched her eyebrows down as she thought about this. *Maybe I need a disappearing spell. To make that wall disappear.* Her thoughts were muddled and confused. No words came.

The memory of the chest in the attic popped into her thoughts. She pushed the leaves away from the hollow place between the roots of the willow tree. She lifted the chest out. *Yes. I'm right. This one is just like the one in the attic. Can I open this one now?* She rubbed her fingers across the side. There was an invisible lock. *Maybe my key will unlock it.* She raised her hand and wished. The key appeared in her hand, and the lock became visible. She unlocked the chest and lifted the lid.

A stretchy pink cap lay inside the chest. She picked it up and looked at it. It was soft and fuzzy. It felt like a silly thing to do, but she pulled the cap on her head. It fit her. She patted the side of the cap and closed her eyes.

A voice said, "I am your thinking cap."

"What?" Her eyes popped open. "Who said that?" She looked behind her to see who had spoken. No one was there. She removed the cap and examined it. It looked ordinary. She lifted the cap, hesitated and then put it back on.

"I am your thinking cap. I belong to you now."

She smiled. *I'm magic*, she thought. *And now I have a magic thinking cap. Good.* The leaves of the willow tree quivered above her head, letting in flashes of shining light. *This is a magic place. It is my secret place. I can think about things here.*

She wondered if her thinking cap could help her remember. The cap's warmth radiated down into her heart. She spoke her questions out loud. "Who is on the other side of this forgetting wall? Why didn't my remember spell work?"

Her thinking cap was silent. No answer came.

"Why won't you answer me? What good is a thinking cap if it doesn't help you think?"

"Think about what you do know," said the cap.

Maybe if I had a picture, it would help. That thought reminded her of Aunt Lillian and the library. The rest of the house was always tidy and neat because Aunt Janet insisted it be that way. But the library was Aunt Lillian's room. The books she liked to read were stacked on the small table by her comfortable chair or in a haphazard tower on the floor. Mary Alice was always welcome to join her in the library. They would look at books together or just sit quietly while they each read a book.

Yesterday Aunt Lillian had been looking at a photograph album—at least that's what it looked like. The large blue book was open on her lap. It had pictures in it. The book was closed very quickly when her aunt saw Mary Alice. Aunt Lillian smiled nervously and said, "I didn't hear you come in. Did you need something?" Her voice sounded almost normal, but her face seemed sad.

"Is that a picture album? Can I see?" Mary Alice had said.

"Not now, child," her aunt replied. And then she began coughing—hard. "Will you go get me a glass of water?"

Mary Alice ran to get the water, but she paused just outside the door. She peeked back inside. Her aunt was not coughing anymore. She watched Aunt Lillian slip the album behind some books on the bottom shelf. When Mary Alice returned with the glass of water, Aunt Lillian was sitting in her chair and the book was gone. Nothing more had been said about that secret book.

The memory of that book faded as she heard someone approaching the willow tree. The footsteps stopped and she heard a voice. *That's Aunt Janet. Who's she talking to?* Maryalise parted the branches slightly. Her aunt was standing by a large thistle plant. It was tall with bushy, prickly leaves. The purple bud on the top was just starting to open. *That thistle wasn't there yesterday. I would have seen it. How did it get that big so fast and why is Aunt Janet talking to it?*

"Thistle, how came you here? What message will you bring?" Aunt Janet reached out with her finger and touched the thistle bud. "Thistle, do thou guard this garden well?"

What? Aunt Janet talks to a thistle plant? How strange.

Aunt Janet started back toward the house, stopping along the way to stare at the muddy flower beds. Maryalise let the branches fall back into place. *Oh no. I've got to get back to the house before she does. I have to be Mary Alice now.*

She quickly put her thinking cap away and hid the treasure chest. Then she crawled out of her secret place. She wiped her muddy hands on her dress. Bending low, she ran around the edge of the garden toward the house. The mud was slippery and felt squishy between her toes.

When she reached the porch, she quickly wiped the bottom of her feet on the mat. Retrieving her shoes from behind the flower pot, she slipped into the house. She intended to go upstairs. However, she glanced toward the library and remembered Aunt Lillian's book. *I wonder what's in it*, she thought as she detoured into the library. Kneeling down, she quickly removed the books on the bottom shelf and looked into the opening. *Nothing. There's nothing here. Aunt Lillian moved it. Why?* She frowned. *Why did she hide the book from me?*

She was putting the books back on the shelf when she felt a tiny pulse of magic. *There's magic here. I can feel it.* She reached out her hand and her fingers felt what her eyes could not see. *It's there. There's an invisibility spell.* The magic was stronger now that she was touching the book. *Aunt Lillian has magic?* Mary Alice wished she could make the book visible, but she didn't know how to undo a spell that had been cast by someone else.

Since she couldn't pull it out, she felt all around the book. Her fingers touched something caught between the book and the wall. By wiggling her fingers, poking and reaching she was able to capture that something between two fingers and pull it out. It was a picture. *It's them. It's a picture of the three girls who came to my secret place. They all look like each other. And they look like me.*

She turned the picture over. There was writing on the back: "We three sisters, Annie, Flora, Denelia."

But who is who? Mary Alice wondered. She looked at the picture again. The girls were standing in front of this house. *When were they here?*

She heard the outside door open and shut. *Oh no! Aunt Janet.* Mary Alice was afraid that she would be scolded for something. While her aunt entered the kitchen, she used the skirt of her dress to wipe up the mud where she had been kneeling. She tiptoed up the stairs, carefully avoiding the squeaky step. After she slipped into her room, she closed the door.

She sat down on the side of the bed and gazed at the picture. The squeaky stair creaked. Someone was coming up the stairs. She quickly slipped the picture inside a book. *If that's Aunt Janet, she'll scold me for sure.* But it wasn't that aunt. It was Aunt Lillian who came into the room.

"Goodness sakes, where have you been?"

"In the garden," Mary Alice replied as she stood up.

"I can see that." Aunt Lillian pointed to the mud on the front of her dress.

"Oh, no. Aunt Janet will be mad."

Aunt Lillian pulled the dress over Mary Alice's head. "This dress is certainly a mess."

"I know." Mary Alice stared at the skirt of her dress. She didn't want to explain how it got so muddy. "But can you get it clean again?"

"Possibly. I'll try. Right now you need to get ready for breakfast. You can wear your brown dress." Her aunt smiled. "I'm supposed to be waking you up, and here you've already been outside and back in again." Her words sounded like a scold, but the tone of her voice was soft, and she had an amused smile on her face.

Mary Alice pulled her brown dress over her head. She grabbed the blue dress from her aunt and wiped most of the mud off her legs and the top of her feet before she pulled on her socks. As she put on her shoes, she said, "Aunt Lillian, where are the pictures of me when I was little?"

Her aunt stopped in the doorway. Her hand reached out and grasped the door frame as if she needed its support. There was a soft gasp and then the silence hung between them. When Aunt Lillian glanced over her shoulder there was an odd expression on her face. At last she said, "You want to see your baby pictures?"

Mary Alice nodded.

"Child, they're. . . they're gone." Aunt Lillian looked as if she wanted to say something more, but she didn't. "Hurry child, you need to go downstairs for breakfast. Right now."

Mary Alice followed Aunt Lillian down the stairs. *Shall I show Aunt Lillian the picture? Will she tell me who the girls are? I'm not sure*, she thought as she started down the stairs. *Should I show Aunt Lillian the picture*? she wondered again. *No, not yet. She might take it away.*

The Locked Door

Questions whirled around inside Mary Alice's head as she entered the kitchen*:* *When did they live here? Why did Aunt Lillian hide the picture album? Why won't anyone talk about them?* Aunt Janet was already sitting at the table. Golden rays of sunlight danced through the window, filling the room with light. Tiny specks of dust in the air danced like little fairies, but Mary Alice was so preoccupied with her thoughts that she didn't pay any attention to them. A bowl of oatmeal was set at each place on the red-checked tablecloth. *I hope it's not lumpy*. It was Aunt Janet's turn to cook this morning. When she cooked, they sometimes had to eat lumpy oatmeal. When Aunt Lillian cooked, they had pancakes or waffles.

Mary Alice sat down. She picked up her spoon and waited until Aunt Lillian was seated before she began to eat. But she didn't really notice what she was eating because she was thinking about those girls. *I know they lived here. They were standing in front of this house in the picture. Annie's notebook is in the attic.* Thinking about that notebook, she said, "Annie. . ." She had not meant to speak out loud.

"What?" said Aunt Lillian. Her eyes looked confused and sad. She started coughing and her face got red.

Aunt Janet froze. A stunned expression flickered in her eyes and vanished. Mary Alice wasn't sure if she had really seen it. That startled look was followed by a quick, angry glare at her sister. Then her gaze returned to Mary Alice. Her aunt's face became hard, and stern lines settled across her forehead "What did you say?" she demanded.

"Oh nothing," Mary Alice said. "I was just thinking." She really hadn't intended to ask yet and hadn't thought how to ask. However, since she had begun, she plunged on. "I was just wondering about Annie, Flora, and Denelia. Who were they and when did they live here?"

Aunt Janet's eyes flashed. There it was again--that quick darting look at Aunt Lillian—an angry look. Then that glare was focused on Mary Alice again. "You need to stop pretending and imagining things. You're a little too old to have imaginary friends."

Aunt Janet's words hurt. *Why does she always criticize me?* Mary Alice looked down at her lumpy oatmeal. When she replied, her voice was soft and hesitant. "But I didn't imagine them. They are real. They were here." She paused and silently stirred her oatmeal. Then she continued. "I'm not sure when they were here. But I found Annie's notebook in the attic."

Aunt Janet looked over at her sister once more with that quick, darting glance. Then she looked at Mary Alice again. "And who gave you permission to play in the attic?"

When she realized how upset her aunt had become, Mary Alice wished she had never said anything. She didn't want to answer that question. Aunt Lillian looked worried. Mary Alice didn't like it when Aunt Janet was mad at her sister. Aunt Janet might be even madder if she knew that Aunt Lillian had said she could play in the attic. "I. . . . I. . . . I" stammered Mary Alice. "I couldn't go outside because it was raining, and so I thought. . . I decided to play in the attic." She looked right at her aunt. "That's when I found the notebook. It's Annie's. She wrote it." Her words tumbled out faster now. "I think Flora, Annie and Denelia are sisters. I thought maybe you might know who they are."

Aunt Janet momentarily seemed to forget that she had said the three girls were imaginary friends. "Just what did the notebook say?"

"Not much. Not enough. Most of the pages were ripped out. I'll go get the notebook and show you." Mary Alice pushed her chair back from the table and stood up.

Aunt Janet's eyes now mirrored the anxious expression in Aunt Lillian's eyes. When she spoke, her voice was sharp. "Mary Alice, you haven't finished weeding yet. You were told to do that two days ago. I want you to go right now!"

Mary Alice was startled at the abrupt turn the conversation had taken, but she wasn't about to argue. So she didn't say anything. She turned and went out the door.

She stood on the porch and thought about her aunts and their unexpected reactions to her questions. It was mysterious—very mysterious. *Why won't they talk about those girls? Why are they so worried? And what are they worried about?*

She stared at the garden. Mud, sticks, and leaves covered the paths. The flowers were beaten down and covered with dirt. Aunt Janet had forgotten about the storm and the mess in the garden. She didn't usually forget anything. Aunt Lillian hadn't remembered either. *I'd better go talk to Aunt Janet,* Mary Alice thought as she turned to go back into the house. *She scares me when she's mad.* She didn't want to talk to her aunt right now—but felt that she must. She slowly opened the door a crack and listened. *If she's still mad, I won't go in yet.*

She could hear her aunts talking. Aunt Janet was saying, ". . . spells and imagining magic must stop."

Aunt Lillian never argued with her sister, but now she said, "Janet, you cannot change what is within her—an integral part of her. You cannot forbid her to be what she is."

The tone of Aunt Janet's voice changed. It almost sounded like pleading. "I just want to protect her."

"I know. I understand, but I feel that we will protect her best by acknowledging the magic that is within her. We need to help her be the best that she can be."

Aunt Lillian knows I have magic? And protect me from what? Monsters? Dragons? The woman on the dragon? She shivered when she remembered the dark dragon and its rider. *Aunt Janet will keep me safe. She promised.* That thought felt very comforting. Deep inside there was a knowing, a feeling that this was right. But at the same time, she felt there was a different name for Aunt Janet that she should remember. She waited for the name to come, but that tantalizing shadow of a memory faded before she could retrieve the name. *I really need that remember spell.*

Her aunts' voices were quieter now, and she could not hear their words clearly. She opened the door a little wider and it creaked. It wasn't a loud noise, but it was loud enough. The conversation in the kitchen stopped abruptly.

When she opened the door the rest of the way, Aunt Janet frowned at her. "Mary Alice, what are you doing now? I sent you out to weed. You can't have finished already."

Mary Alice whispered, "I. . . I can't weed anything. The garden is full of mud and sticks and leaves."

"Of course, how could I have forgotten that?" Aunt Janet's laugh sounded fake. "We'll just have to clean the garden up again, won't we?"

All that day Mary Alice was kept busy. She gathered leaves and sticks and dumped them on the pile of weeds behind the garden shed. There was a rotten smell back there, and she felt uneasy when she had to go near the pile of weeds. Her mind was busy thinking as she washed the mud off the stepping stones in the garden paths.

She thought about her aunts' odd reaction when she had asked about the three girls, and she puzzled over the notebook in the attic. *A magic spell brought the words back to the page. Would they still be there? Would the notebook have answers?* Carrying another bunch of sticks to the weed pile, she thought, *Is the notebook safe?* She stood still and thought, *Why did I think that? Of course, it's safe. It has to be safe.*

Mary Alice remembered the notebook and its torn pages. The pieces of paper had swirled like snow, and words had appeared on the page. Then Aunt Lillian had called her to come eat. She recalled her actions. *I put the notebook back in the chest and closed the lid. I locked it with the golden key. I whispered a protecting spell so no one else can open it. I hid the chest under the blankets. It's safe. Of course, it's safe. It has to be safe.*

It was a long afternoon. Every time she thought she might slip up to the attic and get the notebook, one of her aunts was upstairs, or they had a new job for her to do. She was afraid to ask if she could go get the notebook because she was sure that Aunt Janet would probably say no. When it was time to go to bed, the notebook was still in the attic. It was early and the sun had not gone down, but she had to go to bed anyway.

She lay in bed and thought about the three sisters. The light in the room began to fade. She knew that on the other side of the house her aunts would be sitting on the side porch. They would watch the creeping shadows grow longer and they would smile at each other as everything turned a lovely golden color and the fiery red sun slipped behind the mountains.

Mary Alice usually sat on the side porch with them and watched the sunset. It was their special time of day. If she coaxed, Aunt Lillian might tell stories. Aunt Janet never did. Sometimes they would simply sit in silence or they would talk about their day and make plans for tomorrow. They were often still talking when the night surrounded them, and the stars twinkled above them. However, tonight Mary Alice had been sent to bed early with no explanation. *Maybe they didn't want me to ask any more questions*.

She was still awake when the light faded and darkness filled her room. She listened to footsteps come up the stairs. Her door opened. She closed her eyes and pretended she was asleep. *If they don't want to talk to me, I don't want to talk to them.*

Aunt Lillian slipped through the door, tiptoed across the room and smoothed the covers over her. Mary Alice felt the whisper of a kiss on her cheek. Then she felt a gentle touch on her shoulder and a second whisper kiss on her cheek. She opened her eyes just a little. Aunt Janet was there, too. Mary Alice was surprised. It was usually just Aunt Lillian who tucked her in. *I'm really too old for that, but Aunt Lillian likes to do it.*

She smiled as her aunts left the room. She listened as one door and then the other door was shut. Outside her window, a chorus of frogs and crickets sang their night-time song. An owl called "whoooo" as it swooped overhead on silent wings.

One bright star appeared in the sky. It was the wishing star. She slipped out of bed and tiptoed over to the window to look at the night sky. Her eyes closed as she whispered her wish. "I want to know more about those three girls." She leaned her arms on the window sill, resting her chin on them and continued thinking. *Why do I look like them?*

More stars flickered into sight. Magic surrounded her, and she became Maryalise. Now she could feel the magic grow stronger. Countless stars smiled down at her. A mystic wind carried the song of the stars down to her as she looked at the silvery Milky Way. She smiled. *It's a pathway to the stars. I could follow it. I could dance with the star fairies.* She imagined twirling and dancing and singing a song of joy and gladness high in the heavens. The stars' music enticed her and invited her to come. *I could go up that silver path, but I won't. I'm needed here.*

Her thoughts returned to the notebook in the attic. *Maybe I can get it tomorrow. But I want it tonight.* She tiptoed back across the room and got her flashlight from the table by the side of her bed. Although she could probably cast a spell for light, she decided that she wouldn't use magic since she had a mortal device that would work. Darkness hid her as she cautiously slipped down the hall toward the attic. She did not turn the flashlight on until the door at the end of the hall was safely closed behind her. Arriving at the top of the steep, narrow steps, she discovered that the attic door wouldn't open. It was locked.

She sat down on the top step to think. *Aunt Janet doesn't want me to be in the attic. She doesn't want me to have Annie's notebook. Why?* She could not think of any explanation. *Did Aunt Janet lock this door? Will my key unlock it?* She lifted her hand, invoked the spell, and the golden key appeared in her hand. She stood up and turned around. Focusing the flashlight's beam on the lock, she attempted to insert the key into the keyhole, but it would not go in. Holding the flashlight steady, she looked into the keyhole. She could not see anything but blackness. The keyhole was empty.

I guess my key only opens the chests, she thought as she put the key away. She reached out her finger and touched the keyhole. There was a jolt of magic. Someone had placed a magic lock on the door.

She thought longingly of the notebook as she trudged back down the stairs, and tiptoed down the hall to her room. *Why were my aunts upset when I found the notebook? Why did someone put a magic lock on the attic door? Who locked the door?*

She cautiously closed her bedroom door and climbed back into bed. *Was Annie's notebook still in the chest?* Sadness flowed into her heart because the notebook was lost to her. However, as her head touched the pillow, she had a new thought. She sat up again. *I couldn't undo the magic lock on the attic door. Maybe no one else can remove my protection spell. Annie's notebook is in the chest. It's safe.* She lay back down. *It's safe. It has to be.*

She closed her eyes and went to sleep.

Nurturing

It's a perfectly beautiful morning, thought Mary Alice. A teasing breeze whispered in her ears as her feet danced down the garden path. She had been sent to weed the daisies. However, the sunshine and the flowers beckoned to her. *I'm going to weed the daisies. I really am. But first I need to make sure the flowers are all right.* With that thought, she became Maryalise once again. Her heart felt light and happy. *I did a healing spell yesterday. Did it help?* She saw that the garden was beginning to look like a rainbow of blossoms once more. The song of the flowers floated on the breeze. She loved the song that they were singing. *They sing because they are happy. But why do I hear them? Does Aunt Lillian hear them too?*

She smiled and nodded her head at the pansies. She watched a blue butterfly flying above her. It fluttered down and landed on her fingers before it winged its way skyward. *My healing magic worked.*

This morning Aunt Lillian had said it was beautiful in the garden and that the flowers were perking up. But Aunt Janet had just said to weed the daisies. *I'm a nurturer.* Aunt Lillian often said that a nurturer plants seeds and cares for her growing plants. Maryalise liked feeling that she could do that. She danced past the daisies. Tall stems climbed toward the sky in spite of the clumps of crabby grass that was trying to choke them. "I'll be back," she promised them.

She stopped when she reached the thistle plant, and she became Mary Alice once more. The thistle plant was even bigger than before. "I guess the growing spell helped it, too," she said as she touched the thistle bud with one finger. A warm, happy feeling—a good feeling—spread from her finger, up her arm, and into her heart. Her forehead wrinkled as she tried to understand what was so special about this thistle plant. *A thistle is a weed. Isn't it*?

Earlier that morning, as she put her breakfast dishes in the sink, Aunt Janet had said, "Mary Alice, today is a good day to weed those daisies. The garden is not so muddy now, and the soil is moist. That will make it easy to pull the weeds."

Mary Alice thought about her dandelions. She never pulled them. "There are dandelions in the garden," she said. "Do I have to pull the dandelions? I like them."

"No, child," her aunt said. "You may leave the dandelions. Although most people call dandelions weeds, in this garden, they are not."

"What about the big thistle plant? Shall I dig it up?"

A horrified look appeared on Aunt Janet's face. "No, leave it alone. Leave it alone."

Mary Alice was surprised, but before she could say anything, Aunt Lillian spoke. "Leave the thistle, child. Janet likes thistle flowers."

Now she studied the thistle plant. She walked all the way around it and looked at it from all sides. Why is this plant so important? She shrugged her shoulders. "Oh well, I guess it's time for me to go weed those daisies."

She often worked in the garden with Aunt Lillian. Her aunt loved flowers, and she taught her niece to recognize each one. Aunt Lillian explained about the language of flowers. Each flower had a meaning and you could give someone a message by giving them a bouquet of flowers. Mary Alice enjoyed looking up their meanings in *The Language of Flowers* book. Aunt Lillian usually kept this book on the nightstand by her bed. She did not mind if Mary Alice curled up on the bed and looked at it.

Sometimes they brought the book down to the library and looked at it together. That was one of the special times they shared.

Mary Alice walked back down the garden path toward the daisies and softly named each flower she saw. She named their meanings too. "Pansy, remembrance. Lily of the valley, faith and loyal love. Violet means faithfulness." Passing the marigold, her nose wrinkled at its strong scent. "Marigold means pain and grief."

She paused by the rose arbor and said, "Roses are for love—all kinds of love." New growth was visible at the end of each brittle stem and one bud was starting to open. She waved her hand above it and around it. "Grow in peace," she whispered. Thinking about that thistle plant once more, she thought, *I wonder what Aunt Lillian's book says about thistle flowers.*

She continued thinking about flower meanings as she knelt and began pulling the weeds that choked the daisies. *Daisies mean a lot of things-- - loyal love, purity, faith, cheer, simplicity.*

Her fingers stopped pulling weeds as she continued thinking. *Just look at all these weeds. No wonder Aunt Janet wants me to weed the daisies. The crabby grass and these other weeds will choke the daisies if I don't pull them.* She was sure that the daisies would be happy when all these weeds were gone.

Mary Alice was doing more thinking than weed pulling. A worm wiggled in the little hole where a weed had been. She picked it up and laughed as it wiggled and tickled her hand. She became Maryalise as she lifted it up and spoke to it. "This is my garden. Weeds don't belong here. Little worm, I command you to send those weeds away."

"Mary Alice! For goodness sake!" It seemed as if Aunt Janet was right behind her. "You're twelve now. That's too old to be talking to worms!" Being Maryalise slipped away. She hung her head and slowly turned. She expected to meet her aunt's angry stare. But no one was there.

But I heard her. At least I thought I did. Mary Alice frowned as she looked around the garden once more. Her aunt wasn't anywhere in sight

Aunt Janet doesn't understand me. She doesn't understand me at all. I guess I imagined her voice. But that's what she would have said.

The worm continued to wiggle in her hand. She smiled and became Maryalise once more. Lifting the worm up, she whispered, "Did you hear what I said? I am Maryalise. I have commanded you to send the weeds away."

The worm wiggled again but didn't reply.

Of course, it didn't. It's only a worm. She laughed as she placed the worm down and watched it wiggle down into the moist soil. "I wish you really could talk to me. You could tell me what it's like down there under the ground."

What if I really could talk to the worms? And the birds? I'd like talking to the flowers. Her fingers closed around more weeds as she whispered, "I wish the flowers could talk to me."

"No, don't," said a tiny voice. It wasn't very loud, but it was clear.

She looked around to see who had spoken. There was no one there.

"Don't pull." said the voice, "Not weed. Daisy."

I didn't think that. And I didn't imagine it either. She looked down at the clump of weeds she had started to pull. The stem of a pink daisy had been grasped along with the clump of crabgrass. She opened her hand. The daisy bobbed up and down. It seemed to be thanking her. She reached out one finger and touched the daisy.

"Thank you," Daisy said.

She leaned closer. "I didn't know flowers could talk."

"Didn't ask. Didn't try."

She wondered if all the daisies could talk. She looked at a yellow daisy. "Hello," she said. The daisy didn't reply. "Can any of the other daisies talk?" she asked Pink Daisy. There was no answer. She reached out her finger and touched the daisy again.

"Have to touch," Pink Daisy said.

She touched the yellow daisy. "Hello."

"Hello, Maryalise," said Yellow Daisy.

What? No one knows my secret name but me. "You know my name!" she exclaimed.

"See you, watch you."

Maryalise touched a white daisy before she spoke. "Hello, White Daisy."

"Help me. Pull weeds."

She could barely see the white daisies among the weeds that surrounded them. She began pulling weeds rapidly. She was careful to not pull the daisies. As the weeds piled up on the garden path, she could see more daisies. *It does look better when the weeds are gone*, she thought.

Now she could see that there was a new flower among the daisies. It was yellow with little red streaks. Although it looked like a sweet pea she knew that it wasn't. *I wonder what kind of flower you are.* She reached out and touched it. "Who are you?"

The flower did not answer.

Why doesn't it talk? Aunt Lillian will know what it is. She became Mary Alice once more. She could hear Aunt Lillian singing. "Be happy sings the little bird on boughs beneath the blue." That was the song her aunt sang when she was happy. Mary Alice picked a blossom from the new plant and followed the sound of that song.

"Be happy, happy all day long and others will be too." There was a bench by the rose arbor where Aunt Lillian often sat. She rested and looked at the garden and sometimes she hummed that song, and sometimes she sang it. Today Aunt Lillian wasn't resting. She was using a small gardening shovel to dig up the weeds by the roses.

Mary Alice held the new flower out. "Aunt Lillian, look. I found this flower. What is it?"

Her aunt looked up. The rest of the song vanished as the color drained out of her face. "Where did you find that flower?" she demanded.

"In the daisies."

Aunt Lillian pushed herself up from her knees. “Show me.” She followed Mary Alice back to the daisies. The new flower seemed taller. Mary Alice wondered how it grew so fast. The plant’s leaves seemed to reach out as if they would grasp the daisies.

Aunt Lillian gasped. “Bird Claw, you evil plant. By what magic did you come here?”

“What? It came by magic?”

Aunt Lillian coughed, and her face turned red. She seemed nervous. “I think of this plant as evil because it sneaks into a garden. It grows very fast.” She frowned. “Because it has pretty flowers, people don’t realize it’s a weed. So they leave it in the garden, and then Bird Claw crowds out the flowers. It grows over the top of them and smothers them. It is evil. Evil.”

“What did you call it?” asked Mary Alice. Her aunt’s reaction to this plant made her uneasy.

“It is actually a plant called bird’s foot, but I name it Bird Claw. Look at the seed pods.” She pointed to the seed pods but did not touch them. They were brown with streaks of red.

Mary Alice leaned over and studied the seed pods. “They do look like a bird’s claw. Let’s pull it out.” When she grasped the stem there was a sharp, prickly sensation in her hands. She jerked her hands back. “Ow!” She looked for thorns or stickers. She could not see any, but something had hurt her hands.

“Let me see,” her aunt said. She examined Mary Alice’s hand and then gently rubbed it. Warmth seemed to push the pain away.

“I’m all right now,” Mary Alice said. But she thought, *How did she do that?*

“Leave it alone. Don’t touch it,” said Aunt Lillian. “Let me do it. We have to dig Bird Claw out. His tap root can go deep into the ground. We must get rid of every piece.” When she had finished digging up the weed, she reached into the pocket of her gardening apron and took out a pair of small garden clippers. She began to cut Bird Claw into very small pieces.

"Fetch me a bucket from the garden shed," she said. Mary Alice hurried to the shed and returned with the bucket. Aunt Lillian carefully picked up all the pieces of the weed and placed them in the bucket. "Leave it here," she instructed Mary Alice. "Don't touch it."

Mary Alice watched her walk quickly toward the house. *I didn't know she could move so fast.*

In a few minutes, Aunt Lillian came back. She was carrying a carton of salt. She opened it and poured salt into the bucket. "This will kill Bird Claw," she said, "and keep the pieces from sprouting and growing a new plant." Her aunt carried the bucket over to the garden shed and dumped the dried and shriveled remains on the pile of weeds behind it. Mary Alice watched from a distance. She never went behind the garden shed unless she had to. There was always a rotten smell back there and today it seemed stronger.

"Come," said Aunt Lillian, "we've done enough weeding for today." She walked briskly toward the house, but she didn't look back to see if Mary Alice was following.

I have to think about this. Flowers that talk. Evil weeds. And why did Aunt Lillian act so strangely? Becoming Maryalise, she slipped down the garden path to the old willow tree, parted the branches and crawled into her secret place. She brushed the leaves aside and uncovered the treasure chest. When she lifted her arm and invoked the magic spell, the golden key appeared in her hand. Once the chest was opened, she took out her thinking cap. Pulling it down around her ears, she thought, *I wonder who this cap belonged to.*

"Denelia," said a voice inside her mind.

The voice was so clear that Maryalise answered out loud. "Who did this chest belong to?"

"Denelia."

Maryalise was delighted. She was glad to have someone answer her questions. "Who does the key belong to?"

"Denelia first, and now you," said the voice.

"What about the chest in the attic? Who does it belong to?"

"Denelia. Annie gave it to Denelia."

Maryalise remembered that the chest in the attic had a notebook in it. She wished she had that notebook right now. But she remembered that the attic door was locked. *Maybe I can summon it.*

She thought carefully about the words for a summoning spell. She wanted to use rhyming words so the spell would be powerful. The notebook was in the chest in the attic, but she couldn't think of any words to rhyme with attic. So she needed to think of another way to say it. When she thought of the right words, she spoke them aloud, slowly and with power.

> Annie's notebook, Annie's notebook,
> I summon thee.
> From out of the attic,
> From out of the chest,
> I command that you come to me.

She sat with her eyes closed, and rested her hands on her lap, palms upward and waited. She felt a shiver of excitement, a magical feeling in the air. When she opened her eyes, she expected to see the notebook, but her hands were empty.

"Mary Alice, Mary Alice." It was Aunt Janet's voice. She didn't sound angry or mad this time. She sounded frightened.

"Mary Alice, where are you?" That was Aunt Lillian's voice, and she sounded frightened, too.

What's the matter? thought Maryalise. *I'd better go find out.* She became Mary Alice as she took off her thinking cap. She opened the chest. Annie's notebook was inside. She reached out her hand and touched the notebook. *It's really here. It came. I wish I had time to read it.* But she didn't. She placed her thinking cap on top of the notebook. Then she closed and locked the chest. *I'll come back later and read it.*

She crawled out from the shelter of the willow tree on the far side, and when she was far enough away, she stood up and called, "Here I am."

"Where were you?" said Aunt Janet. Her mouth was fixed in that angry straight line, but her eyes looked worried. "Why didn't you answer when we called?"

Mary Alice hung her head. "I'm sorry."

"It's time to come in the house," said Aunt Lillian. She didn't say anything else but her eyes looked worried too.

"I'm sorry," Mary Alice said again. She was sorry she had worried her aunts, but she was even sorrier that she didn't have time to read the notebook.

Annie's Notebook

When Mary Alice woke up, she could hear a little bird outside her window. She yawned and stretched her arms above her head. Sunlight streamed across the room and warmed her face. It seemed to be welcoming her to a new day. She sat up in bed and immediately thought about Annie's notebook. She wondered what was written in it. *I will go out to the willow tree and get it right after breakfast. I just have to know what that notebook says.* She dressed quickly and went downstairs.

She smelled the sweet aroma of pancakes and warm syrup as she entered the kitchen. It was Aunt Lillian's turn to cook.

Even though she was eager to go out into the garden, she ate three pancakes. "Thank you, Aunt Lillian," she said as she finished her last pancake. She put her plate in the sink and turned to go outside. "I saw some crabby grass—I mean crabgrass in the snapdragons," she said to Aunt Janet. "Would you like me to pull it out?"

Aunt Janet glanced at her sister.

Aunt Lillian looked back. Her smile changed to a worried frown.

Aunt Janet said, "Mary Alice. . ." She paused and then said, "There's a lot to do in the house today. Lillian cooked breakfast. So I'll wash the dishes and you can dry them."

Mary Alice was disappointed, but she didn't say anything. She dried the dishes as quickly as she could, but her aunt was being slow and methodical. *I can't dry dishes that haven't been washed yet. She might get upset iff I tell her to please hurry. She'll wonder why I'm anxious to weed the snapdragons.* Finally, the last dish had been dried. Mary Alice hung the wet dish towel on the rack and turned to go outside.

"Mary Alice," said Aunt Janet, "I want you to dust the library."

Her feet slowed. "Today? Right now?"

"Today. Right now."

"Aunt Janet, there's an awful lot of crabgrass in the snapdragons, and it's crowding them out. It's growing taller all the time."

"Dust the library," said her aunt. The set of her lips told Mary Alice that there was no use arguing.

Mary Alice knew there were a lot of things in the library that needed dusting. She considered using a magic spell. Then she could go read Annie's notebook. She shook her head as she slowly walked out of the kitchen, across the hall and into the library. *No. Not a good idea. She'll get mad if I use magic. And I don't want her to know I have magic.*

After the dusting was done, Mary Alice had to wipe fingerprints off the woodwork in the kitchen. *I think Aunt Janet just doesn't want me to go outside today. Why? Aunt Lillian was upset when she saw that Bird Claw weed. Is that why? But that doesn't make sense. It's gone now.*

The morning crept slowly by. One task followed another. Aunt Janet was always working nearby. There was no time when Mary Alice could slip out into the garden.

After lunch, Aunt Lillian said, "Mary Alice, let's go weed those snapdragons. I'll help. The job will get done faster with the two of us working together." Mary Alice hurried out the door. Aunt Lillian was right behind her. Mary Alice thought, *Now I'll be stuck pulling weeds around the snapdragons. I want to read Annie's notebook.*

She looked longingly toward the willow tree as she walked over to the snapdragons. She grabbed a handful of crabgrass and pulled. She stared at the roots and thought, *I don't think my aunts are going to let me be alone in the garden today. Annie's notebook might as well be locked in the attic.*

She was kept busy all afternoon. Evening came and still she had not found a moment to slip out to the willow tree and get the notebook.

The golden sun slipped down behind the mountains. Mary Alice sat with her aunts on the side porch. They watched gold and red streak across the sky. Dusk began to settle on the house, and deep violet shadows crept across the grass.

Although Mary Alice was tired, she didn't want to go to bed. Since she couldn't read Annie's notebook, she wondered if her aunts would answer some questions. She sat very still as she pondered which questions she might ask. *If I ask about those girls, I might get sent to bed now. I can't ask about the magic lock on the attic door because I don't know who put it there. Every time I ask about Bird Claw, Aunt Lillian coughs and changes the subject.* Then she got an idea.

"Aunt Janet, Aunt Lillian, I was wondering. . . Where is my mother? And my father? I can't remember them. Why can't I remember them? I do have parents, don't I?"

"Child," said Aunt Lillian. She began to cough and her face got red. "Child," she said again and coughed some more.

Aunt Janet said, "Of course you have parents. They are traveling right now."

Mary Alice leaned forward. "Traveling? Where? And why can't I remember them?"

Aunt Janet paused. She seemed to be searching for the right words. "I can't tell you."

"What!"

"We're not allowed. . . We can't tell you anything. It will be better if you remember on your own."

This didn't make sense. "Have I been sick? Did I have a terrible accident? What happened?"

Aunt Lillian said, "Child, we can't tell you. It will be better if you remember on your own. Be patient."

"And now," said Aunt Janet, "it is time for you to go to bed."

Mary Alice stood up and stalked toward the door. She turned and stared at her aunt. "Nobody ever tells me anything."

Aunt Janet stared back. "Mary Alice. Go to bed. Now."

She glanced at Aunt Lillian.

"Just go," Aunt Lillian said.

"It's always time for me to go to bed when I ask questions that they don't want to answer," Mary Alice muttered as she stomped up the stairs. "Nobody tells me anything," she repeated as she attempted to go to sleep. However, sleep didn't come because her mind was too full of questions.

She heard the squeaky step groan as someone came up the stairs. Her door opened, and Aunt Lillian slipped into the room. "Be patient, child," she whispered. "Be patient."

Mary Alice did not look at her aunt. *I hate being patient. I want to know now.*

After her aunt left the room Mary Alice slipped out of bed and tiptoed over to the window. A pale moon sent silver beams of light down into the garden. The willow tree shimmered in the moonlight. *I wish I were down there right now. Maybe I could summon a moonbeam and slide down into the garden.* She thought about that possibility, but she wasn't sure she could really do that. Maybe she could tiptoe downstairs and quietly slip into the garden to get the notebook. But sometimes the door squeaked. So that wasn't a good idea.

It felt hot in her room. She pushed the heavy window up and propped it open with the board that was always left by the window. She crossed her arms on the window sill and rested her chin on them. The scent of jasmine drifted up to her. She knew there was a jasmine vine with tiny white flowers that climbed the trellis by the corner of the porch. She looked down at the porch roof just outside her window. *It's perfect. I can climb down the trellis. The aunts' rooms are across the hall. They won't hear or see me.*

There was a chair near the window. She picked it up and placed it in front of the window, being careful not to make a sound. Stepping onto the chair, she glanced over her shoulder to be sure her bedroom door was shut. Then she climbed out the window and inched along the porch roof until she reached the trellis.

Mary Alice lay down on her stomach and scooted backward until her legs dangled off the edge of the porch. Her legs swung in and out, trying to find the trellis. One bare toe and then another found the trellis. It swayed back and forth as she inched her way down. *I hope it doesn't break. I don't want to fall.* She hesitated for just a moment and then she continued her careful descent. The sweet smell of night-blooming jasmine was stronger now. She touched one delicate white blossom and leaned closer to smell its sweet fragrance.

"I bring you warning," said Jasmine. "Do not trust Snapdragon. She appears to have a generous nature and a unique beauty, but deception is also a part of her nature. Do not trust Snapdragon."

Mary Alice was no longer surprised that flowers could speak. She stopped climbing. "Thank you," she said. "I will remember your warning."

The flower continued speaking. "You may trust anything that Violet tells you. She is true and faithful. Lily of the Valley is loyal and will always tell you the truth."

Jasmine seems to know a lot of things. Can she answer some of my questions? "Tell me about Bird Claw." she said. And why was Aunt Lillian afraid of him?"

"Bird Claw was spy—pawn of the Evil One. That weed wished to betray you and your magic. He was driven by desire for revenge."

"Revenge for what? Because we killed him? And who is the Evil One?"

"That I cannot say. Always guard against the evil one's spies. Some weeds are just weeds, but others would do you harm."

"But. . . . but, how will I recognize which ones are spies?"

"You have a gift. It is a special gift. You can feel magic. Whenever there is magic present, you will feel it. Use that gift wisely."

Mary Alice now understood how she had known there was a magic lock on the attic door, why her hands stung after touching Bird Claw's stem, and how she had found both of Denelia's chests. "Thank you," she said. "Thank you for telling me." *What else might she be able to tell me?* She tried to think of all the questions that Jasmine might know the answer to. "Why does Aunt Janet like the thistle plant? Who am I?"

"That is all that I will say. I bring you warning. Do not trust Snapdragon. She appears to have a generous nature and a unique beauty, but deception is also a part of her nature. Do not trust Snapdragon."

"I won't," Mary Alice promised. She carefully felt for the next toehold as she continued her climb down the trellis. Annie's notebook was in her secret place and she was going to get it. As she slipped down the garden path, her mind was busy trying to sort out the jumble of questions and answers and more questions. *I have a magic gift. I am magic! Who is the Evil One? How did Bird Claw get into the garden? I have a magic gift. I have a magic gift.*

The moon cast a silver beam along her path. She wanted to talk to Violet and Lily of the Valley, but they were closed for the night. She promised herself that she would talk to them in the morning.

She parted the willow branches and crawled across the white stones. The branches swung back into place. It was dark under the willow tree. When she raised her hand and invoked the magic spell, her golden key appeared. It glowed and filled her secret place with light. She uncovered Denelia's chest and unlocked it. Reaching in, she lifted the notebook. "I won't even open it," she said, "because, if I start reading now, I won't want to stop, and I need to get back to my bedroom before I am missed."

She crawled out from under the willow tree and hurried back to Jasmine and the trellis by the porch. Clutching the notebook in one hand, she took hold of the trellis with the other. "Jasmine, I can't do it," she said, "I can't climb the trellis with only one hand." Tears of frustration welled in her eyes. "How am I going to get the notebook back up to my room? I need both of my hands to climb the trellis and I don't have a pocket in my nightgown. If I try to carry it in my mouth, it might get wet and wash away some of the words." Jasmine didn't answer. Remembering, she reached out her finger and touched a blossom. "How can I get the notebook up to my room?"

"Use your magic."

"Of course," she said. "Thank you, Jasmine." If she had thought about it before, she could have used magic to summon Annie's notebook, and then she wouldn't have needed to climb down and back up the trellis. *But then I wouldn't have learned that I have a magic gift. So I'm glad I didn't think of summoning the notebook.* She brushed the tears from her eyes before speaking her spell.

Notebook of Annie's,
Hear what I've said.
Notebook of Annie's
Fly to my bed.

Although the spell rhymed, it didn't seem very poetic. But it worked. The notebook floated out of her arms and up through her window. She followed it as quickly as she could. When she climbed back through the window, Annie's notebook was lying on her pillow.

A Thump in the Night

Mary Alice settled herself on her bed, picked up the notebook and opened it, but she couldn't make out the words in the dim moonlight. It really was time to go to sleep. She sighed. Slipping the notebook under her pillow, she laid her head on the pillows. *It's here! Annie's notebook is right here.* It was impossible to sleep. She just had to know what was in that notebook.

She thought about turning on the light. But if she did, her aunts might see light coming from the crack under her door. She thumped her pillow and felt the notebook. Looking at the table by her bed, she saw the silhouette of her flashlight. She smiled. Holding her flashlight tightly, she scrunched down in her bed and pulled the covers over her head. Sliding the notebook into her blanket cocoon, she turned on the flashlight, opened the notebook and began to read.

This is my diary. It is a secret diary. Magic protects it. No mortal will be able to find it. No mortal will be able to read it. My name is Annie.

She smiled. "The words are still there," she whispered to herself. She turned that page and continued reading.

This is the record of the magical adventures of we three sisters—Annie and Flora and Denelia. We are magic. Each of us has a special magic. Together our magic is powerful.

They have magic. Mary Alice grinned. *I'm magic, too. Jasmine says my gift is that I can feel magic and recognize when it is there.* Mary Alice read all the words on the second page. At the bottom it said,

We sit down in a circle—Flora, Denelia and I. We reach out and grasp each other's hands and feel the magic move around the circle. There is magic here—powerful magic. The magic grows stronger as we chant our secret names. No one knows our magic names but us. I am. . .

Holding her breath, she turned the page, wondering if the words that had appeared magically would still be there. "Yes!" She smiled. "They're still here." She whispered the last words from the previous page again, "I am. . ."

The next word was blotted out with heavy black ink. There was a small blank space and the printing in the next entry was different.

It is dangerous to let anyone know our magic names. This is Annie's notebook. We are taking turns writing in it. My name is Flora. My flower identity is Peony. We each have a flower identity. I am Peony.

We have each chosen a flower to represent us and our purpose. I am the protector. I protect the garden and my sisters.

Annie's flower is the Snowdrop. She is the one who is loving and keeps us happy. Mama says she is a nurturer. Denelia's flower is the Dandelion.

I'm not sure why, Mary Alice thought, *but I am linked to these three sisters by some special, magical knowledge.* Flora continued:

Denelia plans to be a traveler and a messenger.

Wow!

Mary Alice turned the page. The handwriting on the next page was different.

I am Denelia. I plan to be a traveler. Right now I am a messenger, a giver of information. My sisters and I think that we should write our story. So I will start at the beginning.

Mary Alice turned the page. It was blank. *I want to read Denelia's story,* she thought. As she ran her fingers down the page, she felt a hint of magic. Perhaps there really were more words here and they were invisible.

I need a spell. And it needs to be a good one. I'm not sure I can undo someone else's spell. She scrunched her eyebrows down and tightened her lips as she carefully considered her words.

Invisible words,
I feel you here.
I command you now
To reappear.

Words appeared one by one as if written by an invisible hand.

Our mother's name is Elena. She is a mortal. Our father is a fairy. His name is Hawthorne. On the day that he first saw Elena, he was enchanted by her beauty and kindness. He loved her and she loved him. So they married here in this Mortal Dimension—without even thinking that maybe they needed permission from the Fairy Queen. When he took her with him into the Fairy Realm, the Fairy Queen was very angry, and she threatened to banish him from the Fairy

Realm, but our mother pleaded so beautifully that the Fairy Queen relented.

"However," she said, "you and your family must be tested. You will have three daughters, all born on the same morning. When they are twelve years old, they must go to the Mortal Dimension and live there. They will have no memory of the Fairy Realm. When they are old enough to decide, they may choose whether they wish to live as mortals or as fairies."

They'll choose to be fairies. That's what I would choose. Mary Alice continued reading.

It was as the Fairy Queen had said. We three sisters were born on the same morning. On our twelfth birthday, Hawthorne brought our mother and us here to the Mortal Dimension. He placed a spell of protection on this house and the garden. He created a portal between the Fairy Realm and the garden so that he might visit our mother and see us, but he was forbidden to let us see him.

Just before Hawthorne left, the Fairy Queen came to our garden. She had grown to love our mother, but the decree of a Fairy Queen must not be changed. She touched our mother's hand and said, "Elena, care for them well. When they are grown, you will also be allowed to choose whether you wish to live in the Fairy Realm or remain in the Mortal Dimension."

Then the Fairy Queen kissed each one of us, and that kiss caused us to forget our life in the Fairy Realm. We know the story of what happened in the garden because the flowers whispered the story of the Fairy Queen's kiss. That was after we discovered that we had magic.

Mary Alice paused to think. She smiled as she thought about the three sisters. She was glad that they had written their story in Annie's notebook.

I talk to the flowers, too. And she continued reading. The handwriting had changed again.

This is Flora. It is my turn to write a part of our story. At first, we did not remember our life in the Fairy Realm, but our magic together was stronger than the forget spell placed on us by the Fairy Queen. We began to remember.

We learned that we could do magic. Denelia could think messages to Annie and me without saying anything out loud. Annie could put broken things back together. She could heal damaged flowers and injured animals. I discovered that I could use my magic power to protect us from wind, rain, and hail.

We placed a circle of stones around our secret place beneath the willow tree. Then I cast a magic spell on the stones and commanded them to keep intruders out. I devised a magic spell that keeps Denelia's chests safe. She has two chests. The first one is kept in our secret place in the garden and the one Annie gave her is kept in the attic. They are locked with a magic lock, and they can only be opened by Denelia's golden key.

Mary Alice was surprised. She sat up in bed. *I have that key. How did I get it? Why do I have it*? Now she wanted to look at the key again. She raised her hand to invoke the magic spell, and her flashlight rolled off the bed. It hit the floor with a loud thump. The light flickered and went out, leaving the room in shadowy darkness.

She leaned over the edge of the bed and fumbled her hand around, seeking the flashlight. There was a faint noise from across the hall.

Oh, no. She sat very still and listened. There was the sound of soft footsteps coming across the hall. She snatched the notebook and shoved it under her pillow. She lay down with her back to the door and lay very, very still. Someone came into the room and stood by her bed. She kept her eyes closed.

Gentle hands pulled the comforter up around her neck and smoothed her hair. *It must be Aunt Lillian.* She waited for her aunt to go back to her room, but her aunt didn't leave. She stood beside the bed for a long time before she turned and walked toward the window. Mary Alice opened her eyes a very little bit. The light from the moon fell on her aunt's face. It isn't Aunt Lillian, she realized. *It's Aunt Janet.*

She watched as her aunt ran her fingers all the way around the window. She placed her hands on the window and murmured something very softly. Mary Alice heard the sound of her aunt's voice, but could not distinguish the words.

Aunt Janet turned, and Mary Alice quickly closed her eyes. The sound of footsteps moved towards the door. Then they stopped. Mary Alice opened her eyes a very little bit once more. Her aunt bent over and picked up the flashlight. Carefully placing it on the small table beside the bed, she murmured, "So this is the thump that woke me up." Then Aunt Janet went back to her own room.

Mary Alice waited a long time. When she felt that she simply couldn't wait any longer, she cautiously reached out her hand and felt until she touched the flashlight. She pulled it under the covers and clicked it on. Nothing happened. She wiggled the switch back and forth. Nothing happened. She shook it. The light would not turn on.

"Oh, no," she sighed. *The bulb's burned out. Aunt Lillian has some new ones downstairs, but I'm supposed to be asleep. I'll have to get one from her tomorrow.* Mary Alice climbed out of bed and slipped the notebook under her mattress. She thought the words of a magic protecting spell and hoped it would work even though she hadn't said a word out loud.

Magic here in the night,
Hide this notebook from all sight.

I'll have to read the rest of the notebook in the morning, she thought sadly. Her mind was full of the three sisters and their story as she drifted off to sleep.

The Power of Three

Mary Alice opened her eyes. The shadowy grayness that filled her room told her it wasn't the middle of the night, but it wasn't quite morning either. She felt excited and couldn't go back to sleep. She wondered what was so special about this morning. It was in that moment which divides the dark from the dawn that she remembered. *Annie's notebook. I have to read the rest of it!*

She slid out of bed and pulled the notebook out of its hiding place. Sitting on the floor, she rested her back against the bed and cradled the notebook against her chest. Outside her window, the sun's golden light chased the shadows away. A ray of sunshine beamed into her room. She smiled and opened the notebook. She turned the pages until she found her place. Once again the handwriting had changed.

This is Annie. It is my turn to write. I want to write about the night we finally saw our fairy father. We watched the moon come peeking over the hill. It was pale and seemed to have a silver halo all around it. Shimmering beams of moonlight made a pathway from the sky down to the earth, and the moonbeams seemed to be dancing in our garden. As we looked out the window, it seemed to us that the stars were singing, and they called to us to come and play in the garden.

We climbed out the window. One by one we climbed down the trellis. We were Snowdrop, Peony and Dandelion, and we wanted to dance in the garden in the moonlight.

This was their room. Mary Alice glanced at the window and then began reading again.

Jasmine first spoke to us that night. We had not known that flowers could talk. We soon discovered that Jasmine was a teller of secrets. She said, "There is a portal here in the garden. Your father placed it here."

We were surprised. Our mother had often assured us that we had a father, and she said that he loved us very much. But she would not tell us where he was or why he was not with us. When we pleaded and begged, she would say, "I cannot tell you, but you must believe me. He loves you very much, and he would be here with us if he could.'"

Since our mother would not—or could not tell us, we asked Jasmine. "Tell us, Jasmine," we said, "where is the portal? How do we open it?"

"How it opens, I know not. But he comes when the round moon is high in the sky. He comes from another dimension. He speaks with your mother in the moonlight. He dances with your mother in the moonlight. He looks in your window as you sleep, and his tears fall like rain. Then he goes.

How it opens, I know not. But he comes when the round moon is high in the sky." Her voice went on and on, saying the same words over and over again. Jasmine was not only a teller of secrets—she was also a repeater of secrets!

Mary Alice paused and looked toward the window. *Yes! That's exactly what Jasmine is—a repeater of secrets.* Mary Alice continued reading.

We decided that if we wanted to know more, we would have to see that portal for ourselves. The next night was the night of the full moon. When our mother tucked us into bed, we pretended to go to sleep. She tiptoed in and watched us for a long time. We lay very still. When she was convinced that we were asleep, she left our room.

Then we slipped out of bed and tiptoed over to the window. Flora cast an invisibility spell for us, and we stood at the window. We watched the moon rise. When the moon was high in the sky, the portal opened.

First, we saw a small circle of light, and, as we watched, it grew larger and larger. We looked through the opening, and we could see misty colors and golden light. A tiny figure flew through the portal and into our garden. He had transparent wings that looked like silvery-green leaves. We watched as he folded his wings and became larger. Our mother ran to greet him.

"Hawthorne, you are here."

He folded his arms around her. "Oh, Elena. You are as lovely as ever."

He was so handsome. We looked at each other and smiled but did not speak a word. We watched as they laughed and talked and danced in the moonlight.

When Hawthorne looked up toward our window, we backed away even though we believed that he could not see us. We scrambled back into bed and pretended to sleep. Suddenly Flora sat up in bed. "The invisibility spell. I almost forgot about it." She removed the spell and snuggled back down under the quilt. It would have been awful if he saw an empty bed.

From outside the window, we heard our father whisper, "You are so beautiful, so precious, my daughters. Goodbye, my sweet ones. I love you." Then he flew back down to the garden, and we heard him speak to our mother in the garden, saying again those words. "They are so beautiful, so precious. Take good care of them."

We slipped out of bed and peeked out the window once more. He was in his fairy form—no more than three inches high. He flew around our mother. His wings were silver in the moonlight. He kissed our mother on her cheek as the portal opened. Then he turned and flew into that circle of light. The portal closed and he was gone.

Oh, thought Mary Alice, *I wish that I could peek into the Fairy Realm, too.* She continued reading. The handwriting had changed, and Denelia continued writing their story.

One peek into the Fairy Realm was not enough. We were determined to see it for ourselves. We began trying to think of the words for a magic spell. We wanted a spell with words that rhymed because we had learned that rhyming spells are better.

Mary Alice looked up and smiled. *I've learned that too. Spells with rhymes work better.* She was anxious to find out what happened. Her eyes returned to the words in the notebook.

So we thought of a magic spell. The next night we waited until we were sure our mother was asleep. We slipped out of bed and climbed down Jasmine's trellis.

We stood in the center of the garden and joined hands to form a circle. We chanted together:

> We are the three—the power of three.
> Together we call on the powers that be.
> Open the portal—open it wide,
> Doorway to dimensions on the other side.
> We are three—the power of three.
> Together we call on the powers that be.

We watched the portal open. First, we saw the tiny circle of light that got bigger and bigger. Misty golden light poured through the portal into the garden. When the mist cleared, we saw a tiny garden. A crystal waterfall splashed into a silver stream. The song of the stream drifted out through the portal. There were flowers sprinkled across the grassy meadow.

We saw butterflies of every color fluttering from flower to flower. Annie was the first to realize they weren't butterflies. She let go of my hand and pointed. "Look," she said. '"Look. They're fairies." We saw them for only a moment before the portal shimmered and closed.

Mary Alice closed her eyes and tried to imagine what the Fairy Realm looked like. *I can see it perfectly! It's just the way Denelia described it.* It was almost as if she could remember it. *But I've never been there before! Or have I? I just don't know.* She opened her eyes and turned the next page. Denelia was still writing.

We couldn't forget how beautiful the Fairy Realm was. All that next day we would look at each other and remember, and then we would smile and laugh. Our mother asked us what was so funny, and we wouldn't tell her. We gathered in the attic for a private talk. Flora devised a spell that cast a circle of silence around us so no one could hear our words. "We have to go there," I said, "we have to open the portal and go in." Flora and Annie weren't so sure.

"What if we can't come back?" Annie said.

"Do you think Hawthorne will be angry?" Flora said.

"We just have to go," I said. "I can't stand it if we don't go in." I would not give in. I pleaded and begged until I convinced them. We have decided that we will attempt to enter the Fairy Realm tonight when the moon comes out.

At first, we thought maybe we should destroy this notebook so no one could learn its secrets if we didn't return. I ripped out a page, and I slowly tore it into tiny pieces. We watched the pieces fall into the notebook. Ripping up our story gave me an awful feeling inside.

Flora said, "Wait! Don't! Let's make the words invisible."

Mary Alice turned to the next page. It was empty and the rest of the pages were empty. There were no more words. *What happened? Something interrupted them. I guess they didn't have time to make the words on the first pages invisible. Or something went wrong with the spell.* Mary Alice clutched the notebook to her chest as she tried to imagine what had happened. Someone had to put the notebook in the chest. And someone locked it. Then it was hidden under the blankets. Mary Alice thought about this and decided that it was probably Denelia who hid the notebook because she was the last one to write and the chest belonged to her.

Mary Alice wished there was a way she could talk to the three girls. Maybe she could summon them. She considered carefully. If this was going to work she had to get the words of her spell right. Finally, she spoke the words.

Annie, Flora and Denelia,
Please come to me.
Tell me please,
What did you see?

Mary Alice waited. And waited. No one came. Her magic was not strong enough. Or her spell was not good enough. She wasn't sure. She couldn't stop thinking about the three sisters. *Did they go to the Fairy Realm?* Since her spell would not work, she tried to summon a picture of them in the garden when they opened the portal. No picture came. She became Maryalise and tried thinking of an uninvisibility spell.

Words on the page, hidden from me,
Cancel the spell of invisibility.

Nothing happened. The pages remained empty.

Cancel, oh cancel the invisible spell.
I need to see the words very well.

Nothing happened. The pages remained blank. She rubbed her fingers lightly across the pages and felt nothing. She rubbed her fingers across the pages again and again. The words weren't there. No one had written anything else. *If there were more invisible words here, I'd feel them. I can feel magic.*

Maryalise sat thinking for a long time. She slowly closed the notebook and slid it under the mattress. *How can I find out what happened? How can I bear not knowing?*

She sat and thought for a long time before an idea occurred to her. *Denelia's thinking cap! Maybe it can tell me*. She jumped up. Becoming Mary Alice, she pulled on her dress. She hadn't done any chores yet today, but she wondered if Aunt Janet would let her go into the garden anyway. *Maybe I won't ask. If I don't ask, she can't say no.*

She quickly finished dressing and ran into the hall. Standing at the top of the stairs, she listened. Since there was no sound coming from the kitchen and she couldn't see anyone downstairs, she climbed onto the banister and slid down. It was almost like flying! *How would it feel to actually fly*?

Her feet hit the floor and she ran past the kitchen, and out into the garden. She hurried down the path toward the old willow tree. When she reached the daisies, she stopped. *Maybe the flowers knew what happened.* She crouched by the daisies and reached out to gently touch the petal of a white daisy. "Good morning Daisy," she whispered. "Do you know if Flora, Denelia and Annie went through the portal?"

"Don't know. Portal?"

"The portal was in the garden. Did those three girls go through the portal?"

"Don't know."

Mary Alice sighed. She asked again. It was no use. No matter how she reworded the question, Daisy always gave her the same answer. "I'm asking about Flora, Annie and Denelia. Where are they?"

"Denelia gone."

"Denelia is gone? Where did she go?"

"Don't know."

Maybe if I ask about Flora and Annie, Mary Alice thought. But then she realized that there were other voices in the garden. Crouching lower, she listened intently. She heard Aunt Janet's voice.

" . . . . think Thistle is trying to send us a message? Will there be a message here?"

"I don't know, Janet," Aunt Lillian said. "It has been a long time since he disappeared. I wish he would send us a message."

Who was Thistle? It doesn't sound like they're talking about the thistle plant. Mary Alice had come into the garden to get answers and it seemed that she was only going to get more questions. Aunt Janet's voice was coming closer. Mary Alice stayed low. She crawled behind a bush and waited until her aunts had gone back into the house. Then she crept down the path toward the willow tree and stopped to look at the thistle plant.

Who was Thistle? And what message might he send? And why did he disappear? She studied the thistle plant carefully. There was only one bud. It was bigger now, but it had not fully opened. *Can this thistle send messages? Messages from who?*

She reached out and touched the leaf of the thistle plant. She thought it would feel prickly, but it didn't. It was soft and velvety and felt friendly. "Who are you?" she whispered. "Why are you here?" The thistle plant didn't answer. She touched the bud and repeated her question, "Who are you?" But the thistle still did not reply. *I guess buds can't talk.*

Continuing on to the willow tree, she reached the circle of magic stones. Now she felt magic—bad magic. Someone or some evil thing had tried to enter her secret place. She walked all the way around the circle of stones. The circle had not been broken. She crawled across the stones and felt safe. *Whoever or whatever it was couldn't cross the magic circle of stones.*

I'm safe here. My secret place is safe. I can feel good magic here. But something was different. She sat very still and let the sensations of change drift around her. She analyzed the situation piece by piece. Someone had been here. This was the first time since she found this secret place that she was aware that anyone else had entered. She could sense that whoever it was had meant no harm and had no evil intent. She closed her eyes and became Maryalise. She tried to see who had been here.

Who has come into this place?
Let me now see a face.

A picture of Aunt Lillian came into her mind. She saw her part the willow branches and crawl inside. *Why would Aunt Lillian come here? Why?*

Someone in the Garden

Maryalise sat motionless as she looked at the image of Aunt Lillian and thought about her. *What was Aunt Lillian doing in here? I don't mind if Aunt Lillian comes in.* She noticed her aunt was wearing the same blue dress with white flowers that she wore yesterday. She tried to understand what had happened. *After we finished weeding the snapdragons yesterday, Aunt Lillian must have returned to the garden and came here. Why?*

The image of Aunt Lillian continued moving. First she touched each of the stones in the magic circle. When she had touched the last stone, she smiled and nodded her head. Next her aunt crawled over to the tree. She brushed the leaves aside, reached into the hollow and brought out Denelia's chest. Her fingers traced the lock as she held the chest in her lap. *The invisible lock. She knows that it's there. There were tears on her aunt's face. She is crying. Why does Denelia's box make her sad?* The image of Aunt Lillian wavered, and then it was gone.

I don't understand. Maryalise crawled over to the tree, reached into the hollow and brought out Denelia's chest. Lifting her hand, she invoked the spell, and the golden key appeared. After unlocking the chest she took out Denelia's thinking cap. She pulled it on and smoothed it down around her ears.

"There are a lot of mysterious things happening," she said. "And I'm going to figure them out." She closed her eyes and thought about this secret place. *Why did Aunt Lillian come out here? She doesn't have the key so she can't unlock Denelia's chest, but she knows about the invisible lock.* As she thought about Denelia's chest, she had questions she hoped the thinking cap could answer. "Why was I able to see the invisible lock? Why do I have the key?"

The thinking cap was silent.

"Who put the circle of rocks around the willow tree?"

"Flora, Annie, Denelia."

"Who cast a protection spell on them?"

"Flora."

"Something evil tried to come in here? Who was it? Why did it want to come in here?"

The thinking cap did not have an answer for those questions.

Her thoughts moved out into the garden. She thought about the thistle plant and that Bird Claw weed. *Why was Aunt Lillian so upset about it*? Maryalise opened her eyes and looked down at her hands. The prickly red marks were gone. *Was Aunt Janet upset about Bird Claw, too? Is that why she didn't let me come out into the garden by myself*?

"Why can I talk to the flowers?"

The thinking cap did not answer.

I have lots of questions and I need answers, and my thinking cap isn't helping much. She touched her hands to the cap. *I guess it doesn't know everything,* she decided.

She thought about all the questions she needed answers for. She spoke each question out loud and paused after each one—hoping to hear an answer.

There was only silence.

"Where are my parents?

Why can't I remember anything before I came to live with my aunts?

Why do I have magic?"

When she thought about that question, she remembered the attic door. "Who put the magic lock on the attic door? And why? Did someone want to keep me from reading Annie's notebook?"

Maryalise knew that the notebook was proof that Flora, Annie and Denelia were real. *When did they live here? Where are they now?* Then Maryalise remembered something else, *Daisy told me that Denelia was gone. Gone where? And she didn't say anything about Flora and Annie. Why not?*

All those questions were spinning around and around in her head. "I'm going to get some answers," she muttered. "My aunts won't answer my questions. My thinking cap isn't much help. I'll go ask the flowers."

She took off her thinking cap and placed it back in the chest. She locked the chest and carefully placed it into the hollow at the base of the tree. After covering it with leaves, she crawled out from under the willow tree.

When she had crossed the stones, she felt that touch of evil again. A dark shadowy something scurried away. It disappeared so quickly behind the garden shed that she wasn't sure if she had really seen anything. But a nasty smell lingered in the air. She decided to strengthen the magic spell on the circle of rocks. When that was done, she paused by the thistle. Once again she touched its leaves and felt a warm, reassuring feeling. She touched the thistle bud. *It is taking you a long time to bloom.* "Hello, Thistle," she whispered, and she waited. The thistle bud seemed to nod up and down, but it didn't speak.

Wandering on down the garden path, she bent over and touched a golden marigold blossom. "Marigold, can you tell me where Denelia is."

"Gone, gone," wailed Marigold. "I miss her."

"Where did she go?"

"Gone. Gone," wailed Marigold. "Long time gone."

"What about Annie and Flora? Where are they?"

"Gone. Gone. Denelia is gone. I miss her." Marigold sounded so sad, so full of pain and grief.

Maryalise patted Marigold gently before moving toward a small cluster of white flowers. Tiny bells hung from delicate stems. She reached out her finger and touched one of those delicate bells. "Lily of the Valley, tell me about Annie. Where is she?"

"Here."

Maryalise looked all around. There was no one in the garden except herself and the flowers. "Here? There is no one here but me."

"Here. Love Annie. Annie loves. Annie comes here."

This was puzzling. *Lily of the Valley knows who Annie is. She remembers her, but I don't understand what Lily is saying.* She started to walk on but paused to ask one more question. She touched Lily once more. "Do you remember Flora?"

"Comes with Annie. Sometimes. Comes here. Annie comes here."

It's so frustrating. Absolutely frustrating. They know about those three girls, but their answers make no sense at all. Maryalise slowly turned and looked carefully at each flower in the garden. She wondered which one might have more information. She smiled when her eyes saw a big pink blossom. Its petals were soft and ruffly. She ran to peony and cradled the largest blossom in her hands. "Peony, tell me about Flora."

"Flora is brave. Flora protects. Flora keeps us safe."

"But where is she? Where did she go?"

"Not gone. Here."

"Tell me about Annie."

"Comes here."

"Oh!" said Maryalise. She shook her head back and forth. "Look," she said. "There is no one here but me! Why won't anyone give me a straight answer?"

She stomped down the garden path as she tried to make sense of what the flowers had told her. Her leg brushed against a snapdragon. "Denelia is gone," Snapdragon gleefully told her. "Denelia isn't coming back. She doesn't like us anymore."

"What?"

"Denelia left. Long ago she left. Promised to return. But she didn't." There was slyness in Snapdragon's voice as her petals opened and shut. Maryalise didn't say anything. She just listened. "Don't trust Jasmine," muttered Snapdragon. "She loves to talk, but she doesn't know anything. Flora's spells don't work anymore. Annie is careless."

Maryalise stooped down and whispered, "You know about them. Where are they? Please tell me."

Snapdragon waved back and forth on her stem. "Won't tell you. Why should I tell you? I've said all that I'm going to say. Won't say anymore. Don't believe Jasmine. Jasmine doesn't know anything. I've said all that I'm going to say!" Snapdragon's petals snapped shut.

Well, Snapdragon is no help at all. None of the flowers make sense today! I'm not going to get any answers from the flowers. Trying to think who might be willing to answer her questions, she remembered the notebook. *If I read Annie's notebook again, will it help me find some answers?*

When she started toward the house, she glanced at the garden shed. She glimpsed a dark shadow that was there and then was not there. *What did I see? What was that?* Looking at the shed, she noticed a vine climbing up the side of it. *That wasn't there yesterday.* She stopped and thought about that vine. *Well, I don't think it was.*

She ignored the queasy feeling in her stomach and walked over for a closer look. The vine had tiny purple flowers that looked like stars. Small red berries hung from the ends of each branch. She reached out to touch the vine, but a prickly bad feeling made her hesitate. She remembered Bird Claw. And she remembered Jasmine's warning. *Maybe I should wait until Aunt Lillian can look at that flower with me. Maybe it's another bad plant—like Bird Claw.*

She hurried toward the house. The puzzling vine and its star-shaped flowers slipped out of her mind. Annie's notebook might help her solve some of the mysteries she kept discovering. A dandelion seed floated by. She reached up her hand and caught it. When she cradled the seed in her hands, she heard it whisper, "Jasmine. Ask Jasmine. Jasmine knows."

I will. Tonight. When Jasmine blooms again.

There was no one in the hall when she came in the door. She looked at the banister and remembered how much fun it had been to slide down that banister. It had felt almost like flying! Then she remembered, *I can do magic. Can I slide up the banister?* She stood at the bottom of the stairs and touched the banister. She hunted for the right words and then she chanted.

I am magic.
I have magic inside.
I am magic
And up I will slide.

She felt herself becoming lighter and lighter—as light as a dandelion seed floating in the air. Her feet left the ground. She twirled in the air and landed on the bottom end of the banister. Then slowly she began to slide up the banister. When she reached the top, she sat there with a delighted grin on her face. She wanted to save that moment and remember it always.

"Mary Alice. Mary Alice! What are you doing? Get down from there before you fall!" Aunt Janet's angry voice startled her, and she almost did fall. Becoming Mary Alice, she stared into Aunt Janet's angry eyes. "You know better than sliding down the banister!" Aunt Janet said, "Now, go to your room."

Mary Alice slipped off the banister and hurried past Aunt Janet's pointing finger and into her room. She closed the door and leaned against it. *I did it! I slid up the banister. I did it!* She snickered. *Aunt Janet thought I was going to slide down.*

Aunt Janet was muttering something as she stomped down the stairs. Mary Alice opened the door a crack and peeked out. She watched her aunt rub the back of her neck with both hands. She brought her hands around to her forehead and pressed her fingers against her temples. "That child will be the death of me," Aunt Janet grumbled as she went out the door toward the garden. "That child will be the death of me yet."

Oh no. Aunt Janet's getting one of her bad headaches again. And how could I be the death of her? I don't have a gun or a knife. I get mad at Aunt Janet, but I wouldn't ever want to hurt her. Maybe I need to devise a spell to protect my aunts. She nodded her head. *And I will—right after I read Annie's notebook again.* She pulled the notebook out of its hiding place beneath her mattress and wondered, *Will I find answers or more questions*?

Questions

After Mary Alice retrieved the notebook from its hiding place under the mattress, she settled herself on the floor between her bed and the window. If either of her aunts happened to come into her room, she didn't want them to see it. She read slowly this time, thinking about each piece of information. What clues might be hidden in the words?

When she came to the place where Annie wrote about Jasmine, she held the notebook close to her body while she thought about Jasmine. *What do I know about Jasmine?* She turned to the last page in Annie's notebook. She got a pencil and began to make a list:

What I know about Jasmine

Jasmine was a good friend to Annie and Flora and Denelia.
Jasmine told me I have a magic gift.
Jasmine said not to trust Snapdragon.

Mary Alice remembered Jasmine's words. "I bring you warning," Jasmine had said. "Do not trust Snapdragon. She appears to have a generous nature and a unique beauty, but deception is also a part of her nature. Do not trust Snapdragon." She chewed on the pencil's eraser as she thought. *Today Snapdragon told me not to trust Jasmine. Who should I trust?* It was hard to decide. *I'll figure that out later.* She continued writing.

Jasmine told me which flowers I could trust.

Jasmine told me how to get the notebook up to my bedroom.

Jasmine watched them open the portal and peek into the Fairy Realm.

"That's it!" she exclaimed. "I've found my clue!"

The door to her room opened. "Shhh," said Aunt Lillian. "You need to be quiet. Janet has one of her headaches today. I finally convinced her to lie down and rest for a while."

Mary Alice pushed Annie's notebook under the bed and scooted in front of its hiding place. "I'm sorry, Aunt Lillian," she said.

Aunt Lillian looked at her. "You were shouting," she said. "Is everything all right?"

"I'm all right, Aunt Lillian. There's nothing wrong, Aunt Lillian." She didn't want to lie to her aunt, but she wasn't ready to explain why she was so excited. "I'm really all right, Aunt Lillian. I was just thinking about something."

Her aunt's forehead wrinkled, and there was a questioning look in her eyes. Mary Alice waited for her aunt to say something else, but she didn't. She smiled. "Remember to play quietly," she said as she closed the door.

Play? I'm not playing. This is real. Excitement bubbled up inside Mary Alice. She started to laugh, but quickly covered her mouth with her hands. *If Jasmine saw them the night they peeked into the Fairy Realm, did she see them open the portal? Did they go through?* All those questions tumbled and whirled inside her head. *Yes,* she decided. *She probably did because Jasmine blooms at night, and they were planning to try to open the portal after the moon came up.*

Mary Alice's joy turned to despair as she began to wonder, *Can I trust Jasmine? Snapdragon warned me not to trust Jasmine. Jasmine warned me not to trust Snapdragon. Who do I believe? How will I know which flower to trust? Talking to flowers is so complicated. Somebody ought to write a book about how to talk to flowers.* Then she remembered that Aunt Lillian did have a book—*The Language of Flowers*. It wasn't about talking to flowers, but maybe that book could help her.

When she carefully opened her bedroom door, Aunt Lillian was walking up the hall with a cup of tea and crackers for her sister. Mary Alice watched Aunt Lillian went into Aunt Janet's room. Mary Alice thought about that book and wondered where it was. *It's probably in Aunt Lillian's room, but it might be downstairs. Where should I look first?* Mary Alice tried to remember when they had last looked at the book. *I don't know where the book is but maybe the book can find me.*

She said,

Language of Flowers,
Book I want to see.
Wherever you are,
Come to me.

The door to Aunt Lillian's room opened a crack and a thin book floated out into the hall. Mary Alice watched it dip and sway as it moved toward her. She giggled. *I don't think it's had much practice flying..* The book turned and floated through the doorway and into her bedroom. It settled on her hands. "Thank you," she murmured with a smile. "I'll send you back in a few minutes. I know Aunt Lillian won't mind if I read you." *This is silly. Now I'm talking to books.*

She sat cross-legged in the middle of her bed, opened the book and began to read. "The language of flowers, sometimes called florio-graph-y, was a Victor-ian means of communication in which various flowers and floral arrangements were used to send coded messages, allowing individuals to express feelings which otherwise could not be spoken."

As she stumbled over the pronunciation of floriography and Victorian, she decided that it didn't really matter how those words should be pronounced. *I'll skip this part and see what it says about jasmine and snapdragon.* Flipping through the pages, she noticed that the book had information on herbs and weeds as well as flowers. She paused in the weed chapter to look at the picture of bird's foot. *Aunt Lillian called it Bird's Claw,* she remembered. *He's gone now. Aunt Lillian got rid of him.* Mary Alice forgot about him as she continued to turn the pages to find the section on flowers.

When she saw a picture of the new flower that was growing by the garden shed, she paused. The book said that "Bittersweet nightshade is one of the most poisonous plants. It is a vine which scrambles over other plants. The flowers have star-shaped, purple petals and the leaves are dark-green to purplish. The berries are round or egg-shaped and bright red when ripe." She stared at the picture. "That's it," she said. "That's the flower I saw in the garden." *I need to tell Aunt Lillian about bittersweet nightshade.*

However, she did not spend any more time thinking about bittersweet nightshade because she wanted to read about jasmine and snapdragon and the other flowers. She quickly turned the pages of the book until she came to the chapter about flowers. She remembered some of the things Aunt Lillian had told her, but she wanted to know what was written in the book.

She read that "a daisy means loyal love, and simplicity." *Daisy only gives me simple answers.* "Dandelion means 'co-que-try." She stumbled over that word. *What does that mean?* she thought as she continued skimming the pages until she found the entry for jasmine. "Jasmine blooms at night. Jasmine is calming, means feminine kindness, cheerfulness." Mary Alice smiled. *That's exactly how I feel when I talk to Jasmine—cheerful and calm.*

When she continued looking and reading, she found that "lily of the valley means trustworthy, loyal love." She nodded her head and whispered, "Jasmine said I could trust her." She read marigold's information. "The book says that marigold means pain and grief." *I remember how sad Marigold was when she talked about Denelia.*

Continuing to search for information about Snapdragon, she paused to read the information about peony. "Peony means honor and bravery."

She found the page about snapdragons. It said, "Snapdragon means deception, denial, also dignity and unique beauty." She nodded her head in agreement. *Snapdragon is beautiful, but I didn't like listening to her.* She had started to close the book when one more entry caught her eye. "Thistle means nobility." And then she saw a sentence that said: "All winged seeds are messengers." This led her to remember the dandelion seed. It had said, "Ask Jasmine."

I will, she thought. I'll ask Jasmine tonight. *I'm not going to trust Snapdragon.*

When she closed the book she remembered the bittersweet nightshade plant by the garden shed. *I should tell Aunt Lillian*, she thought, *but if I tell Aunt Lillian, she might say I can't go out into the garden. I'll tell her after I've talked to Jasmine.* She spoke a spell and sent the book back to Aunt Lillian's room.

Mary Alice helped Aunt Lillian cook supper. When it was ready, Aunt Lillian sent her upstairs. "Ask Janet if she feels like coming down to eat."

Mary Alice opened the door and tiptoed into her aunt's room. The curtains were closed and the room was dark. A narrow beam of light shone from the hallway to her aunt's face. "Aunt Janet," she whispered. "Aunt Lillian wants to know if you are coming down for supper."

Aunt Janet lifted one arm to shield her eyes from the light. "No child. I don't want any supper. Maybe some tea and toast after a while." When her niece turned to go, Aunt Janet spoke again. "Mary Alice, you must be careful."

Mary Alice stopped. She looked over her shoulder. *Careful about what?*

"Promise me that you will not wander around the house by yourself tonight."

Mary Alice turned to look at her aunt. She didn't understand why Aunt Janet wanted her to promise that. It was an odd thing to ask, but it was an easy promise to make. "I won't." She turned again to go out the door, and she thought, *I can still climb out the window and talk to Jasmine.*

Aunt Janet wasn't finished talking. "Promise me that you won't go into the garden tonight. Promise me that you will stay in your room." Mary Alice could tell by the tone and intensity of her voice that this was important to her aunt. Mary Alice stopped. *How did Aunt Janet know she was planning to climb out the window?* Mary Alice turned and looked at her aunt again. For a long minute, she stood without speaking. This was a harder promise to make. Disappointment welled up inside her. *If I promise, I won't be able to talk to Jasmine tonight. I always keep my promises. If I don't promise, I'll have to explain to Aunt Janet, and I can't do that—not yet.* So she whispered, "I promise." Then she quietly left the room and closed the door.

There was very little said at supper that night. Mary Alice's mind was full of Jasmine and Snapdragon and all the flowers in *The Language of Flowers* book. She kept pushing thoughts of that bittersweet nightshade weed out of her mind. Aunt Lillian seemed to have enough to worry about. Aunt Janet was upstairs in her room, resting in the dark and trying to get over that headache. *Is it my fault that she has a headache tonight*? Mary Alice wondered. *Probably. Aunt Janet gets mad at me a lot. I do things that she doesn't like.*

After the dishes were done, Mary Alice and Aunt Lillian sat on the porch together. A gentle breeze chased the clouds across the sky. One cloud assumed the shape of an almost dragon. The golden sun slipped down behind the hills, causing the dragon to turn pink, then fiery red before vanishing. After the dragon had gone, darkness began to settle over the house and garden.

A small rabbit hopped across the grass, stopping to eat a dandelion. Mary Alice didn't say anything. She reached out, tapped her aunt on the arm, and pointed to the rabbit. The creak of Aunt Lillian's rocking chair ceased as she stilled her chair to watch him eat. Mary Alice knew if they both stayed very quiet, the rabbit wouldn't notice them. She remembered the shadowy thing she had glimpsed in the garden earlier that day. *It could have been a rabbit*, she thought, but deep down inside she knew that it hadn't been. It was something else. "Aunt Lillian. . ." she said. Her voice startled the rabbit. His ears flipped up, and he disappeared into the shadows.

Mary Alice changed her mind. She was enjoying this quiet time with Aunt Lillian. She didn't want to talk about the shadowy thing in the garden right now. "Look," she said as she pointed up into the sky. "Right there. See. There's the wishing star. I get the wish tonight." It was a game she and Aunt Lillian played almost every night. Whoever found the first star was the one who got to make a wish on it. The wishing star glimmered there, a lone star in the darkening night. It was sending is silvery light down, waiting for Mary Alice's wish:

Starlight, star bright,
I wish I may, I wish I might
Have the wish
I wish tonight.

Having whispered the rhyme, she closed her eyes and tried to decide what to wish for. There were so many things she wanted. She finally decided on a very simple wish. *I want to think of the right question to ask Aunt Lillian. It should be a question that she will answer. If I ask the wrong question, I know I'll get sent to bed, and I don't feel like going to bed right now.*

She did not speak as she continued to ponder what that right question would be. She wondered if Aunt Lillian knew Annie, Flora and Denelia. *Or maybe. . . was Aunt Lillian really Annie? If she was, why did she change her name?* But Mary Alice knew if she asked about the three sisters, her aunt would probably cough, her face would get red, and Mary Alice would get sent to bed—again. The stars came out one by one until the sky glittered with stars before she finally thought of a safe question.

"Aunt Lillian, did you live here when you were a little girl?"

"Yes."

"What kinds of things did you do?"

In the darkness, Mary Alice could hear happiness in Aunt Lillian's voice as she answered. "We helped our mother in the house, and we played in the garden. We skipped stones in the pool and waded in the stream." Aunt Lillian rocked gently back and forth. Her face had a far-away look.

Mary Alice leaned forward eagerly. She wanted to ask more questions, but she forced herself to be quiet and just listen. She waited for her aunt to continue.

"On rainy days we played in the attic. We were magic." Aunt Lillian coughed timidly and continued. "I mean, we pretended that we were magic. My sisters and I took turns dancing fairy dances in the attic. I liked to be first. Janet was second and D.. . . ." Her voice faltered and faded away.

Mary Alice waited for her aunt to continue speaking—but she didn't. Mary Alice looked at Aunt Lillian's face. Her smile was gone.

"You have another sister? Besides Aunt Janet?"

"Oh my goodness!" said Aunt Lillian. She coughed nervously before repeating, "Oh my goodness! I didn't realize how late it was getting. It is way past time for you to be in bed."

"Please," said Mary Alice. "Please. Just tell me about your other sister. What was her name?"

"That's enough stories for tonight."

Mary Alice sighed. *Once she sounds that way, there is no way I can out-stubborn her.* Mary Alice sighed again as she climbed the stairs and opened her bedroom door. She put on her nightgown, climbed into bed, and thought about Aunt Lillian as a little girl. *I wonder what she looked like?* Mary Alice pulled the covers up to her chin. *Maybe there's a way that I can see her.*

Becoming Maryalise, she sat up in bed and began to devise a seeing spell. She borrowed some words from a poem she had heard Aunt Lillian say about time turning forward. She changed them a bit and then added two more lines of her own.

> Backward, turn backward,
> Oh, time in thy flight.
> Please turn backward
> Just for tonight.
> Please bring young Lillian
> Into my sight.

It seemed to her as if Aunt Lillian materialized in her room. The shadowy figure was wearing her blue flowered dress. Maryalise watched as Aunt Lillian became smaller and younger.

"Oh," she whispered. "Oh, my gosh! I was right."

She slipped out of bed and took the picture out of its hiding place. They all looked the same. They were dressed alike. They had the same smile. It looked like they were laughing at her. They looked just like Aunt Lillian.

Now I know your secret, Aunt Lillian. You are one of the three sisters. But which one are you? Maryalise remembered the morning at breakfast when she had said, "Annie. . ." and Aunt Lillian had answered.

I think you're Annie.

Maryalise climbed back onto the bed, but she didn't intend to go to sleep—not yet. *I'm sure Aunt Lillian isn't Denelia because she started to say Denelia when she told me about playing with her sisters. And the flowers told me that Denelia is gone. So if she is Annie and Denelia is gone . . .then I think Aunt Janet must be Flora.* This was surprising. It was easier to think of Aunt Lillian being young and dancing like a fairy than of Aunt Janet being young.

It seemed that the shadowy figure of Aunt Lillian was laughing at her.

"I'm right, aren't I? You're Annie."

The shadowy figure didn't answer.

"And Aunt Janet is Flora."

The Aunt Lillian girl smiled but did not answer.

"I know how I can find out for sure," Maryalise said. She scooted to the edge of the bed and chanted the spell once again:

Backward, turn backward,
Oh, time in thy flight.
Please turn backward
Just for tonight.
Please bring young Janet
Into my sight.

A shadowy figure of Aunt Janet in her long white nightgown appeared beside the Lillian girl. Her gray hair became golden brown. She pleated the folds of her nightgown with her fingers and her eyes were gentle—as soft and understanding as Aunt Lillian's. She became smaller and younger. And there she was. The two girls clasped hands and smiled. *Aunt Janet is one of the sisters.*

Maryalise considered what she knew about Flora. She was the protector. *Aunt Janet promised to keep me safe. Aunt Janet is Flora.* Maryalise nodded her head up and down.

But what about Denelia? Where is she? Now Maryalise wanted to see the grown-up Denelia, but she could not think of the words for a spell. "I wish to see Denelia all grown up," she said. But nothing happened. Magic did not summon Denelia. She was gone—just as the flowers had said.

A tear trickled down Maryalise's face as she looked at Annie and Flora. "Where is Denelia?"

The smiles on their faces faded away. "Gone," they said. "Denelia is gone." And they sadly slipped away.

Jasmine

One bright star glimmered brighter than all the others. It was there in the night sky—right in front of her window. None of the other stars were as bright. Mary Alice lay in bed and tried to go to sleep, but her mind was full of Denelia and Jasmine and all those unanswered questions. She tried counting stars, but her mind kept returning to the three sisters. Tonight she had seen Flora and Annie. She had discovered that Aunt Lillian and Aunt Janet were Annie and Flora. *Why wouldn't my aunts tell me who they were?* she wondered. *They were going to open the portal to the Fairy Realm. That's what I wanted to ask Jasmine about. But I can't. When I make a promise I always keep it.*

Now, thinking about her promise, she slipped out of bed and slowly walked over to the window. It was dark in the garden, but that one bright star twinkled at her. It seemed to be whispering "Cheer up. Things aren't so bad."

But they are. Mary Alice sent her thoughts up to the star. *I promised Aunt Janet, and now I'm trapped. I promised her I wouldn't wander in the house by myself tonight. That means I can't go out the front door. I promised her that I would stay in my room tonight. So I can't climb out the window. I need to ask Jasmine about those three sisters and the portal, and I can't! I made a promise, and now I'm trapped!*

Tears welled up in her eyes. She made lots of mistakes, but she had never broken a promise. She wouldn't start now. *But Jasmine's out there, and I'm stuck in here.* Leaning forward, she tried to see Jasmine, but her head bumped against the window, and she felt something. She reached out her hand and touched the window. Next, she ran her fingers around the window. There was magic here. She could feel it all around the window. *It's a spell of protection, but is it here to keep something out or to keep me in? Is this what Aunt Janet was doing the night I dropped my flashlight?*

She knew that the only way she could find out if the spell was supposed to keep her inside was to try to go outside. *I won't really go out*, she told herself. *I'll just see if I can.* She unlocked the window, pushed it up, and propped it open with the board. She carefully placed her chair under the window and climbed up. *Will I be able to climb out?*

She lifted one foot and then she put it back down. *I can't. I want to, but I can't.* Her promise—not a spell—kept her inside. She leaned out the window and tried to see Jasmine. All she could see was the tip of a leaf at the edge of the roof. *I'm keeping my promise. I haven't left my room.*

That one bright star kept twinkling at her. Now it seemed to say, "Cheer up. You'll think of something." A gentle breeze blew hair into her eyes and then meandered on, leaving behind the scent of jasmine.

"I wish I could talk to you, Jasmine. What secrets might you share with me tonight?"

Jasmine didn't answer.

"I know." Mary Alice sighed. "I have to touch you before you can talk to me. And I can't. I wish I could come to you or that you could come to me." She smiled and clapped her hands. "The star was right. I did think of something." She couldn't see Jasmine, but she knew that Jasmine was out there on the trellis. Mary Alice became Maryalise. She looked in Jasmine's direction. She smiled as she chanted the words of her spell.

Jasmine, oh Jasmine,
Don't be slow.
Lift up your leaves
And grow, grow, grow!

She saw a long thin vine began to wend its way over the edge of the porch roof. It grew longer as it crossed the porch roof and waved its way right up to the window and into her bedroom. The vine stopped when it was right in front of her face and leaves began to unfurl one by one. Flower buds appeared and unfolded their tiny white petals. She reached out and touched Jasmine with her finger.

"Hello, Jasmine. Thank you for coming." Jasmine quivered and swayed as if blown by a gentle breeze, but the breeze was gone. Maryalise thought very carefully about what to say next. She didn't want Jasmine to repeat the wrong information over and over again. "Jasmine, what happened the second time that Annie and Flora and Denelia opened the portal to the Fairy Realm?"

Jasmine swayed back and forth. "They came," she said. "They came out of this very window. One by one. My trellis they climbed down to the garden below. Quiet the garden was as the moon came over the mountains and upward into the sky." Maryalise held her breath, anxious to know more. She was afraid to say a single word. *Go on.*

"Annie, Flora and Denelia. They held hands. Made a circle. Words they chanted. I was there. I saw. They came," Jasmine said. "They came out of this very window. One by one. . ."

Maryalise held her frustration and anger inside. She wanted to yell. She wanted to tell Jasmine to stop repeating and go on with the rest of the story, but she knew that wouldn't change anything. She didn't want to make Jasmine angry. She took a breath and waited for a moment. She was careful to keep her voice quiet. "Jasmine, please, what happened? Did the portal open?"

"My trellis they climbed down to the garden below. Quiet the garden was as the moon came over the mountains and upward into the sky. Annie and Flora and Denelia. They held hands. Made a circle. Words they chanted. I was there. I saw."

"Oh, don't stop there," Maryalise wailed. "I want to know what happened. I want to see what happened." Her voice faded away. *It's useless. She's just going to repeat those words over and over again. I wish she could show me.* Maryalise smiled. I could see Aunt Lillian and Aunt Janet. Maybe I can see what Jasmine saw. She voiced her spell.

Backward, turn backward,
O time in thy flight.
Please turn backward
Just for tonight.
Please let me see
What Jasmine saw on that night.

When Maryalise lifted her head, she saw Flora, Annie and Denelia in the garden. Even though she had not left her bedroom, it seemed as if she were in the garden with them. "Hurry," Denelia said, "hurry. The Fairy Realm waits for us." Although the three sisters were identical, Maryalise felt sure that it was Denelia who spoke.

One sister (was it Annie?) reached out and took Denelia's outstretched hand. "Are you sure we should do this?" she asked. "What if we can't come back?"

Denelia laughed. "We have to do this. We'll be together and our magic will bring us back."

The other sister (was she Flora?) reached out to hold Denelia's other hand, and then she clasped Annie's hand, closing the circle. "Do you think we'll see Hawthorne?" she said, "and will he be mad at us if we go into the Fairy Realm?"

"It will be all right," Denelia said. "It has to be all right. I just have to go. I must see the Fairy Realm." Annie and Flora nodded their heads. Now," Denelia said, "the circle of unity is complete. We will say the spell together." The three sisters all nodded. They chanted the spell together.

We are three—the power of three.
Together we call on the powers that be.
Open the portal—open it wide,
Doorway to dimensions on the other side.
We are three—the power of three.
Together we call on the powers that be.

Maryalise watched the portal open. First, she saw the tiny circle of light. She watched it get bigger and bigger. Misty golden light poured from the Fairy Realm, through the portal, and into the garden. As the mist cleared, she saw a tiny garden on the other side. She could see the waterfall and the stream. The meadow was sprinkled with flowers. Tiny fairies twirled in an airy dance above the meadow. It was just the way Annie had described it in her notebook.

Denelia smiled. She let go of Flora's hand. The circle was broken, but the three sisters stood in a row, side by side. Hand in hand they gazed through the portal. Then Denelia let go of Annie's hand. Her excitement carried her forward, and she confidently slipped through the portal. Annie hesitated. Doubt and fear held her back. Flora looked hesitantly around. The portal began to close.

"Wait," Annie called.

"Denelia," cried Flora.

But Denelia did not look back. Flora and Annie stretched out their hands and tried to reach her, but it was too late. The portal had closed. Denelia was gone.

Maryalise blinked her eyes. Annie and Flora were gone. She no longer felt as if she were in the garden. She reached out and touched Jasmine once more. "Jasmine, what happened?" Jasmine was silent. She twisted and slipped away from Maryalise's fingers. She swayed slightly, moving gracefully back through the window and across the porch roof. When she reached the edge of the porch, her tendrils reached down to twine around the trellis. Only the tip of a leaf was visible above the edge of the porch roof. “Wait!” Maryalise called. “Wait! I have to know. Did Denelia ever come back?” Jasmine didn’t answer.

Messengers

After Jasmine left, Maryalise became Mary Alice once more. She closed the window, put the chair back where it belonged, and climbed into bed. But sleep wouldn't come. Thoughts and memories and wonderings jumped and whirled around inside her head. *Aunt Lillian and Aunt Janet are Flora and Annie. I know they are. Why did they change their names? Denelia went to the Fairy Realm. Did she ever return?* Then, thinking about Denelia, Mary Alice thought, *Denelia is their sister. Is she my mother? I look like her. Why don't I remember her?*

She finally drifted off to sleep. Fragmented memories slipped in and out of her dreams—a half-remembered face, a soft voice singing a lilting lullaby, a smile, a warm hug.

Warm rays of sunshine slipped through the window and danced across Mary Alice's face. Their gentle warmth woke her up. She had slept longer than usual. She smiled as she remembered. She had talked to Jasmine. She saw Denelia go into the Fairy Realm. She thought about her dream and felt that it had taken her home to be with her mother. It was as if she had seen her mother, but the memory of that dream was elusive. It hovered just beyond her remembering. This caused her to wonder, *Was Jasmine and the portal just a dream?*

She slipped out of bed and dashed across the room to look out into the garden. The sky was a clear blue and there were no clouds in sight. The golden sun sent its bright rays down to the earth below. White fluffy snowflakes floated above the garden, as silent as a secret wish. *Snow?* Mary Alice blinked her eyes. *Snow? It's not winter.* But the air seemed to be filled with snowflakes. They were dancing, whirling, and hovering in the air. The flowers lifted their faces to the sky, and their song drifted up to her. She lifted the window and propped it up so she could hear the music better. The pieces of white fluff swirled around but did not fall to the earth to cover the flowers. A gentle breeze caught one and wafted it up to Mary Alice's window.

It's not snow, she realized. *It's winged messengers. From the thistle plant.* She reached out her hand. The messenger settled on her palm.

"Tell Denelia," it said.

"Tell Denelia what?" Mary Alice asked.

"Tell Denelia."

It seemed that these were the only words that this particular winged messenger would say. *Maybe the other messengers will say something different.*

She quickly pulled on her dress, but she didn't bother to put on shoes and socks. She ran out of her room and over to the stairs. She didn't look to see if anyone was around as she hopped onto the banister and slid down. She landed with a thump and rushed out the door and into the garden. A winged messenger floated in the air. She lifted her hand, and it nestled into her palm.

"Take care of our daughter."

Another winged messenger drifted down to gently land on her shoulder. "Tell Denelia I'm trapped."

Countless winged messengers floated in the air. Their delicate umbrellas opened wide and a tiny thistle seed swung below each one. Mary Alice turned in circles as she tried to catch them. Every time she attempted to grab one, the wind blew it away. Then she discovered that if she simply held out her hands and waited, a messenger would gently float down. The little seed would nestle into her palms and give its message.

"Don't trust Nightshade."

"Spies in the garden."

"Tell Denelia I love her."

"Tell Denelia."

"Protect garden."

"Magic won't work."

She didn't understand all of the messages, but she gathered as many as she could. After delivering its message, each messenger drifted away. There were so many floating in the air that she could not listen to them all. They floated higher and higher. She watched in frustration as the last of the winged messengers disappeared into the sky above her head.

When she arrived at the thistle plant, one last messenger was still clinging to it. She reached out a finger and touched it. "I bring word from Thistle," it said. Then it released its hold on the thistle plant and floated up, following the rest of the winged messengers into the sky.

Mary Alice wanted answers, and she thought maybe the thistle plant might have them, but it stood tall and silent. There was a new bud, but it was not able to talk because it had not opened yet.

She noticed a small rabbit sitting very quietly by the path. His whiskers quivered. "Hello there," she whispered. "Will you talk to me?" The rabbit's ears flicked upward, and he vanished down his rabbit hole. "I guess not," she said. But maybe the flowers will.

Looking around at the flowers in the garden, she again noticed the bittersweet nightshade vine. *It's a lot bigger today. Why hasn't Aunt Lillian seen it? I need to tell her.* Mary Alice knew if she did, Aunt Lillian might not let her come out into the garden. But if she didn't tell her aunt, the nightshade vine would just keep getting bigger and bigger. She didn't know what to do. *I don't dare let it stay there,* she finally decided. *It might be one of the spies they warned me about. I need to get rid of it.*

She wondered what her aunts were doing. She didn't want Aunt Janet or Aunt Lillian to see her. If they saw her in the garden, they might make her come into the house and do more housework. After casting a spell of invisibility over herself, she marched toward the garden shed. It felt good to know she could do magic even if she was being Mary Alice. The closer she came to the garden shed, the more she felt the presence of evil, but she refused to retreat. She stopped right in front of Nightshade. "You're leaving this garden. Aunt Lillian doesn't want you here. And I don't want you here, either."

Nightshade laughed. It was a hideous laugh.

Mary Alice shuddered.

"Aunt Lillian," he said in an oily snake voice. He laughed again. "She doesn't know I'm here."

Mary Alice could feel his evil power. She jammed her hands on her hips and stomped her foot. "I'll tell her."

"Won't do you any good," taunted Nightshade. "I'm invisible and she can't see me."

This worried Mary Alice. Nightshade's magic was strong. He didn't need to wait for her touch to speak. He could make himself invisible. *And he saw me even though I'm invisible.* Although she wanted to run away, she forced herself to stay. *I'm not going to be afraid,* she told herself. Staring right at Nightshade, she said, "Then I'll get rid of you because I can see you."

"Go away, mortal child," hissed Nightshade. "Your magic may let you see me, but you are powerless to destroy me."

"We'll see about that!" She reached out and grabbed Nightshade. Her hands felt a hundred-thousand prickles poking into them, but she wouldn't let go. She braced her feet against the ground and pulled hard. Nightshade's leaves waved, and he laughed that hideous laugh again.

Leaning backward, she used all of her body weight in an attempt to pull the vine out of the ground.

Nightshade sneered. "Go away, mortal. Leave me be."

Mary Alice let go of the vine. She crossed her arms and leaned forward. "No. I won't!" *Maybe I can destroy him with a magic spell.* As quickly as the words entered her mind she spoke them aloud.

Evil plant that I spy
Your leaves will wither
And will die.

Nothing happened. She squinted her eyes and pressed her lips together as she thought of a different spell.

Magic in me.
Magic I send.
Surround this evil.
Make it end.

Again, nothing happened. She heard Nightshade's evil laugh again.

She thumped her hands on her hips and thought. *Nightshade is really powerful. But I can do this. I can. I just need to think harder.*

Magic in me.
Magic is mine.
Tie in knots
This evil vine.

But no matter how she worded the spell and no matter how many rhyming words she used, her words seemed to bounce off Nightshade.

"Give up mortal child," Nightshade said. His branches waved back and forth maliciously. He seemed larger now. "Your magic is no better than your father's."

"My father? What do you know about my father?"

His laugh hurt Mary Alice's ears. She watched his leaves turn a deep, dark purple. He taunted her, saying, "Your father is Thistle and he lives in a cage. His magic cannot free him." Nightshade lowered his snake voice to a hissing whisper. "Your father has forgotten you. He does not love you."

"That's a lie!" yelled Mary Alice. *My father's name is Thistle? How does he know that?*

"Oh," said Nightshade. "You love your father? Of course. Every daughter loves her father." His vines moved toward her. "Do you want to rescue him?"

She nodded her head.

"Then I can help you." His oily voice became softer as he coaxed. "Tell me your magic name, your secret name, and I will take you to your father."

I do have a magic name. But I'm not going to tell you what it is. There is no way I'm going to give you power over me. However, Nightshade's offer sounded tempting. *I really do want to find my father. I want to remember him.* She considered the offer and tried to think of a different bargain. It was then that she remembered the winged messengers. "Don't trust Nightshade," one of them had said. A second one had said, "Magic won't work."

Mary Alice turned her back on Nightshade. He laughed triumphantly. She stomped around to the door of the garden shed and went inside. The tools that Aunt Lillian had used to get rid of Bird Claw—snippers and a shovel—were exactly where her aunt had placed them. "He says that magic won't work," she muttered. "Well, I am Mary Alice and I will destroy Nightshade. I don't need magic."

She returned and stood in front of Nightshade. "I am Mary Alice," she said, "and I say that you shall not remain in this garden." His branches writhed and twisted as she snipped them off one by one. Her anger kept her from feeling the prickles.

The pile of branches hissed. She reached out with her mind to hear Nightshade's thoughts.

Do what you will, mortal child. My roots are strong. I shall revive and grow again.

"No," said Mary Alice. "No, you won't." She began to dig at his roots with her shovel. The ground was hard, and Nightshade's root refused to let go. She carried water to moisten the soil and continued to dig. When she had finished, she piled the roots on top of the branches. Standing with her hands on her hips, she stared at the remains of Nightshade. "There," she said, "I have destroyed you. You shall not stay in this garden."

His roots thrashed back and forth. His branches hissed, "Oh, foolish child. You know so little." A hideous laugh sounded from each snipped piece. Mary Alice concentrated and his evil thoughts pounded into her ears. The noise twisted inside her head, but she refused to quit listening. Even though she felt dizzy, she focused on separating his words from the noise.

Each piece that you have cut and each root that you have dug shall become a new nightshade plant by the next rising of the sun. All your efforts are in vain for we shall take over this garden.

Tears of exhaustion, frustration, and bitterness slipped from Mary Alice's eyes, making streaks in the dust and dirt on her face. *I'm only twelve, and I don't know what to do next, but I can't let Nightshade win. I wish I had asked Aunt Lillian for help.* Thinking of her aunt reminded her of the way Bird Claw had been eliminated. Now she knew how to destroy Nightshade.

She ran to the house. Her aunts were in the kitchen. Aunt Janet sat at the table. Her head was buried in her hands as she sobbed, "We missed it. Lillian, how could we have missed it? When I woke up, the messengers were all gone. I really thought Thistle would send us a message."

Aunt Lillian patted her sister's shoulder, "Don't worry, Janet. If Thistle has a message for us, he'll find a way to send it."

Mary Alice tiptoed through the kitchen. This was an interesting conversation, but she didn't have time to stay and listen. Aunt Janet looked up. She seemed to have heard something, but she did not say anything. *My invisiblility spell works. Aunt Janet's looking right at me, but she doesn't see me!* Mary Alice stepped into the pantry and picked up a large bag of salt. Turning to go back through the kitchen, she thought, *Oops. What will they think if they see a bag of salt floating through the kitchen?*

She lifted her skirt and wrapped it around the salt. *My underwear is showing, but no one can see it. So it won't matter this time.* She started back through the kitchen. Now Aunt Lillian looked up and listened intently, but she didn't say anything. *Aunt Lillian can't see me either*, Mary Alice thought as she tiptoed past her aunts and out the door. Dropping her skirt, she cradled the salt against her chest and ran down the path to the garden shed. The pile of branches and roots was still there. Nightshade had not yet begun to carry out his evil plan.

"I'm back," she said. "I am Mary Alice, and now I will destroy you." The salt poured down, and Nightshade's branches and roots began to twist and shriek. Mary Alice watched with satisfaction as they became black and brittle. She stared down at Nightshade's unmoving remains. "Nightshade, you have been destroyed, and I didn't need magic to do it!"

The Time of Choosing

Mary Alice smiled triumphantly as she added the dead remains of Nightshade to the pile of sticks behind the garden shed. "There," she said, "that's the end of you." That prickly, ugly feeling near the garden shed was weaker now. However the yucky smell remained, and she felt uneasy. She wondered if Nightshade had been the only spy in the garden or was there another one. The winged messengers hadn't said.

Thinking about the winged messengers caused her to have another question. *Why did Thistle send those messengers?* She did not have an answer, but she intended to find out. Her mind was moving quickly as she went back toward the thistle plant, but her feet were limping slowly. Her feet hurt, and her hands hurt, too. She had ignored the prickles while she was battling Nightshade, but now she felt them.

She stopped and looked at the thistle. *It does look noble—just like Aunt Lillian's book said. It looks determined, too.* Her fingers gently touched the thistle bud. "Hello Thistle," she said. The thistle bud trembled in her hand but didn't speak. "Oh, Thistle, I need answers, and I need them now. I can't wait for you to bloom." *I need a new spell.*

Thistle bud, unfold and grow.
There are things I need to know.

She clasped her hands together as she watched the thistle bud grow larger and unfold. When it was in full bloom, it swayed back and forth on its stalk, as if to tell her that it was ready to talk. She reached out her hand, touched the blossom, and said, "There were winged messengers in the garden. Who sent them?"

"I did," said Thistle. "I sent them."

"I know they were thistle seeds," Mary Alice said. "I want to know who sent them."

"I did," said the voice from the thistle blossom. There was a hint of anger in his voice. "I am Thistle. I am a fairy, and I sent the messages. Who are you, mortal?" She remembered that Nightshade had said her father was named Thistle. *Was Nightshade telling me the truth?* Her mind seemed to remember this fairy's voice and she had a warm feeling in her heart.

"I am. . ." She paused. "I am Mary Alice. Are you my father?"

The thistle blossom seemed to quiver in her hand. When it was motionless once more, it said, "How old are you?"

"I'm twelve." *Why didn't the thistle answer my question*? She asked again, "Are you my father? Aunt Lillian and Aunt Janet won't tell me about my father."

The thistle blossom quivered again. "Yes, Maryalise, I am your father."

Mary Alice was surprised. She knew that she had not spoken her secret name aloud. *If he knows my name, then. . .*

"Where are you, Thistle? I can't see you. Are you invisible? Are you hiding?" Her questions tumbled out one after the other. She looked around to see if she could see her father.

"Don't ask questions," said Thistle. "Just listen. I may not be able to talk long." Although there were many more questions she wanted to ask, she stopped talking and listened.

"I am trapped in an underground cavern. Villiana, the Dark Fairy, has imprisoned me and evil magic surrounds me. I sent a thistle seed to the garden and it grew. I gave words to the winged messengers. Did Denelia get them? Tell Denelia I love her."

"Denelia is gone," Mary Alice said. "She isn't here. I don't know where she is."

The thistle drooped, and a drop of water landed on her foot. She wondered, *Could a flower cry?*

After the plant brought itself erect once more, Thistle spoke again. "You must warn Annie and Flora. Tell them to protect you. Villiana wants you. There is evil in the garden. Beware of spies."

"I found Nightshade. I destroyed him. He prickled my hands and my feet, but I destroyed him. He's gone."

Thistle seemed to gasp. "Nightshade is evil. His poison is in your hands and feet. Go now! Tell Annie to heal you. Tell Flora to protect you, and tell her to guard the garden."

"But. . ."

"Go now!" said Thistle. "This is important. There is no time to waste."

Mary Alice looked down at her hands and feet. Tiny purple lines snaked out from each red prickled spot. Her feet hurt, but she ignored the pain and ran down the path, up the steps, and into the house. Aunt Janet and Aunt Lillian were still in the kitchen when she rushed into the room. "Help me," she cried.

Both aunts turned toward the sound of her voice. "Mary Alice? Mary Alice? Where are you?" They looked all around, but they did not see her.

"Oh," said Mary Alice. "I forgot." She removed her invisibility spell and appeared in the middle of the kitchen. She held out her hands.

All at once there were three conversations happening at the same time.

Aunt Janet wanted to know, "How did you learn an invisibility spell?"

"What happened to your hands?" asked Aunt Lillian.

Mary Alice didn't answer those questions. She said, "I talked to Thistle."

"Where were you?" asked Aunt Janet.

"How did you get hurt?" said Aunt Lillian as she looked at Mary Alice's hands and feet.

"Thistle said to tell Annie to heal my hands and feet," said Mary Alice. "Nightshade prickled them."

Aunt Lillian froze. She didn't speak, but her face rapidly changed from puzzled to angry and then to concerned. She began to gently rub Mary Alice's hands, and she murmured soft, gentle words. Although the purple streaks were still there, the pain subsided and left.

"Do my feet, too," said Mary Alice.

Aunt Janet watched the healing process. Mary Alice looked up at her and said, "Thistle said there is evil in the garden. He said to tell Flora to protect the garden."

"How did—?" Aunt Janet stopped in mid-sentence. "There is evil in the garden?" Without saying another word, she turned and went out the door and into the garden.

During supper, Mary Alice told her aunts about finding the golden key and opening Denelia's chest. She talked about Annie's notebook and the picture and the talking flowers and Thistle and all the other things that had happened. She explained how she had learned that they were Annie and Flora.

She had many questions and she wanted answers, but, every time she asked a question, her aunts just smiled and said, "Later." Mary Alice knew that meant they wanted to talk privately so they could decide how much to tell her.

After supper, they all sat on the side porch. The world was hushed and silent. The golden daylight faded as the last rays of sunshine played across the grass. Purple shadows stretched out their fingers and crept toward the porch. The sky was filled with red and gold.

Aunt Lillian's voice broke the silence. "I think this is the magical time of the day," she said. "I always feel closer to Denelia at sunset. I imagine the pixies and fairies getting ready for their nighttime adventure. They especially like to dance in the moonlight. Sometimes I imagine that Denelia is laughing and dancing with them." Her voice faltered as she whispered, "I hope that she is with them."

Mary Alice held her breath. *Tell me about Denelia.* She didn't dare to ask a single question.

Aunt Lillian rocked slowly back and forth. The rhythm of Aunt Janet's chair was the same. Mary Alice sat on a small stool in front of them and waited. When it seemed that Aunt Lillian had said all she intended to say, Mary Alice reached out to touch her aunt's hand. Her aunts had said they would answer her questions later. Well, this was later and she wanted answers.

"Tell me," she said, "Aunt Lillian, please tell me about Denelia."

Aunt Lillian stopped rocking and looked at her sister.

"Please," Mary Alice said again. "I need to know. Is Denelia my mother?"

Aunt Janet looked back at Lillian and nodded her head.

"Yes," said Aunt Lillian. In that instant, when Mary Alice learned that Denelia was her mother, knowledge came into her mind like a missing puzzle piece that shows up in an unexpected place. She hadn't known who Denelia was a moment before—but now she did. She smiled.

Aunt Lillian reached out and took Mary Alice's hands as she looked into her eyes. "Yes, Denelia is your mother. You have her eyes and her imagination. When you laugh, I hear Denelia's laugh."

Mary Alice sat quietly. She could hear the creak of Aunt Janet's rocking chair. She listened to the first tentative sound of the frog chorus and the faint chirp of a cricket under the porch. Knowing she belonged to someone brought a connected feeling that she liked. She remained silent for a long time, feeling the warmth of love around her. Then she asked, "What happened after Denelia went through the portal?"

Aunt Lillian looked at her sister. Aunt Janet nodded her head once more. "I remember the night that Denelia went through the portal," Aunt

Lillian said. "When the portal opened Denelia was excited. She let go of our hands and went through. I hesitated because I was afraid we wouldn't be able to return."

"I started to follow Denelia, but then I stopped," said Aunt Janet. "I was afraid Hawthorne would be angry. While I hesitated, the portal started to close."

"We watched the portal close," said Aunt Lillian. "We couldn't reach her, and we couldn't stop it from closing. No matter how hard we tried to open the portal again, it remained shut. Denelia was gone."

"And without Denelia's strong magic, our magic was not enough," said Aunt Janet. The magic spell that we had devised was for the power of three, and now we only had two."

Mary Alice looked at Aunt Janet and then at Aunt Lillian. There was a long silence.

"Telling our mother what had happened was very hard," said Aunt Janet. "We were afraid she would be angry with us. We looked at her face and watched a sadness settle into her eyes. 'Hawthorne is your father,' she said. 'He will surely take care of Denelia. She will be safe with him. Perhaps he will bring her back the next time he comes.' A tear slipped out of one eye and trickled down her cheek."

"But he didn't bring Denelia," Aunt Lillian said. "Our mother wasn't angry, but the Queen of the Fairies was. 'The existence of the portal,' she said to Hawthorne, 'brings terrible danger to the Fairy Realm. Once again you have acted with no thought of the consequences.' So the Queen decreed that Hawthorne could not return to the Mortal Dimension until we were old enough to choose whether we would live as mortals or fairies. He might visit our mother one last time, but then the portal would close and remain locked until the time of choosing."

Aunt Lillian leaned back in her chair and sighed. "Those were lonely years. Our mother laughed and played with us, but her smile never made it to her eyes. We often saw her sitting alone in the garden. The pale moon sent down its silvery light, and it fell upon her wet face. Although she loved us dearly, we knew there was an emptiness in her heart that we could not fill. We had the same emptiness in our hearts. We had always been three, and now we were only two.

Sometimes Flora and I would go down to the garden and sit with our mother so she would not be quite so alone. One night, when we were quite grown up, the portal opened. Hawthorne flew into the garden and assumed his mortal size."

Aunt Janet continued the story. "The time of choosing had come. He had come to claim our mother. She could choose to return with him to the Fairy Realm where she would be his soul mate forever.

She did not hesitate. 'Oh, yes. Yes!' she said as she wrapped her arms around him.

Hawthorne turned to Annie and me and held out his hands. 'Come, my daughters,' he said, 'today you are old enough to choose. Come to the Fairy Realm.'

'But what of Denelia?' we asked. 'Where is she?'

'She is safe,' he said. 'There will come a time when she will return to the Mortal Dimension.' He would not, or could not, tell us more about Denelia."

"And so," said Aunt Lillian, "we refused to go. We chose to remain here. Our mother wavered in her decision, torn between her love for us and her love for Hawthorne. 'Go,' we said. 'We have each other. We will wait here for Denelia. If she needs us when she returns, we must be here.' We knew that our parents could return through the portal to visit and we believed that if we waited Denelia would come."

Mary Alice wanted to know more about Denelia. *Did she come? When*? But she willed herself to be quiet and let her aunts finish telling their story.

Aunt Lillian voice became softer as she continued speaking. "Hawthorne held us close and whispered, 'I am proud of you, my daughters. You have made a difficult decision.' He turned and reached out his hand toward our mother. Come, Elena.'

Our mother pressed her wet cheek to ours and kissed us goodbye. Then she reached out and took our father's hand."

The rhythm of her chair stopped. Aunt Janet patted Lillian's hand. Then Aunt Janet leaned forward and looked into Mary Alice's eyes and continued telling the story. "When Hawthorne took our mother's hand, she changed. A bubble of light surrounded her. Her face became younger and softer. Her dress shimmered and fell in soft folds. Iridescent wings fluttered from her shoulders. She was beautiful. We saw our mother in fairy form for the first time. A radiant smile sparkled in her eyes.

We watched as our parents grew smaller and smaller. When the portal opened, they rose into the air and flew into the Fairy Realm. They hovered on the other side, smiling and waving as it closed. Then there were two of us left to sit in the garden in the moonlight."

Mary Alice leaned forward. "But did Denelia ever come back?"

"Eventually," said Aunt Lillian. But not for a long time."

"Why not? The portal was there, wasn't it?"

"That's Denelia's story to tell," said Aunt Janet. She brushed away a tear as she looked out into the darkness. She reached over and took her sister's hand. Mary Alice reached out a hand to each of her aunts. She could feel the magic and the love as it flowed around the circle.

The Forget Spell

Mary Alice and her aunts sat quietly for a long time and enjoyed the feeling of connection. Even after they released their handclasp, the connected feeling lingered. Although she could not recall any specific moments she had shared with her mother, Mary Alice liked knowing that Denelia was her mother.

"Why do I think of her as Denelia? Instead of Mother?"

"Because fairy children call their parents by their given names," Aunt Lillian said.

Placing her fingers against her temples, Mary Alice tried to find a memory of Denelia. "Why don't I remember my mother? I want to remember her, but I can't. The first thing I remember is standing in the garden with both of you."

"It's because of the forget spell," Aunt Janet said.

"What!" said Mary Alice. "You put a forget spell on me? Why?"

"It wasn't me," said Aunt Janet. "My magic was not that powerful. Some mortals may have a little magic, but a mortal doesn't have as much magic as a fairy. A forget spell requires strong magic, and your magic was strong. I couldn't do it. "

"Then who did?"

"Your parents were gone. I promised your mother that I would protect you from Villiana," Aunt Janet said. We, Lillian and I, decided that it would be best if you were hidden as a mortal child. That meant we couldn't let you use magic. We couldn't let her find you." Aunt Janet took Mary Alice's hands once more and looked into her eyes. "You need to understand. Your parents left so suddenly. Hawthorne, our father, had placed spells of protection around the garden many years ago. Thistle added more. I was able to close the hole ripped by Villiana's dark magic. Lillian and I activated Thistle's spells after he was gone. Villiana did manage to force her way in once more, but we have specifically locked her out now."

Aunt Janet's words seemed jumbled and confusing. However, Mary Alice did remember the storm and seeing the dark fairy on a black dragon. *But Villiana didn't see me. At least I don't think she did.*

Aunt Janet paused, took a deep breath and continued, "It was our job to protect you. Villiana is evil and she is determined. Her magic is powerful. She wanted you."

Mary Alice didn't understand. "Why does Villiana want me?"

"She steals magic."

Mary Alice moved a little closer to Aunt Janet. Suddenly she didn't feel quite so safe. She didn't want to hear about Villiana anymore. She gazed into her aunt's eyes and said, "Tell me about the forget spell. Who put the forget spell on me?"

Aunt Lillian interrupted. "It was the forget spell of the Queen of the Fairies. Janet couldn't invoke a forget spell, but she was able to use a spell that transferred all that was Denelia's to you—including the forget spell of the Fairy Queen."

Mary Alice was silent as she thought about this. It explained so much—the chests, the key, and her thinking cap. And she understood why she couldn't remember Denelia. She clasped her hands under her chin. "I wish I could remember my parents. I wish that my magic was strong enough to erase the forget spell."

Wishing can't erase it. But maybe there's another way. Mary Alice clapped her hands together and laughed. "I think I know how to erase that spell. But it will need the magic of all of us. You have to help. Come with me." Without giving her aunts time to reply, she grabbed their hands and pulled them toward the garden. "Come. We have to go to the garden." She stopped in the center of the garden. "Now we need to make a circle of unity—like you did when you opened the portal. I can take Denelia's place." Her aunts hesitated and then clasped hands to complete the circle. Mary Alice closed her eyes and thought for a long time. This spell had to be right. Then she spoke.

We are three, the power of three.
Together we call on the powers that be.
Bring back memories to Maryalise.
We are three, the power of three.
Together we call on the powers that be.

A secret whispering moved through the stillness of the night. A warm feeling of love and happiness enveloped Mary Alice. For just a moment, she felt strong hands touching her shoulder. It felt as though someone was standing right behind her, but, when she looked over her shoulder, no one was there. Fragments of memories and then whole memories slipped into her mind and settled into the place where they belonged. "I remember. I remember," she whispered. "My mother is Denelia and she is a fairy."

She dropped her aunts' hands as she bounced up and down with excitement. "Aunt Lillian, I remember dancing in the moonlight with the pixies and the fairies. It was such fun. Denelia and I danced in the meadow. It was just the way you said. I remember flying. I flew from flower to flower all around the meadow. My mother smiled as she watched me fly."

Mary Alice clapped her hands to her mouth. "I remember my father. His name is Thistle. He is a fairy and he is the Guardian of the Portal."

She smiled as memories of her father filled her mind and heart. "I held his hand and we flew in and out of the crystal drops splashing from the waterfall into the pool. He told me that if I flew fast enough I could fly between the drops and never get wet."

A teardrop trickled down her cheek as more memories returned. "I remember one day there was a beautiful purple butterfly in the meadow. Thistle lifted me up and placed me on its back. The butterfly flew high above the meadow. I looked down and saw my parents smiling and waving at me. 'Hold on tight, Maryalise,' Thistle called."

Mary Alice laughed. "I have a fairy name. Somehow I knew that even when I couldn't remember other things."

The smile on her face faded as darker memories crept into her mind. One day Villiana had forced her way into the Fairy Realm, bringing blackness with her. *Thistle protected me. He wouldn't let her take me.*

After the Dark Fairy had been driven out of the Fairy Realm, her parents had brought her through the portal.

Aunt Lillian smiled, "I remember that night—the night you came to us. There was a full moon. Flora and I were waiting the garden because Denelia was coming to visit us. After our parents left, we had hoped and waited for her to return, and she did. She was a beautiful fairy, but we were still mortals. Thistle came with her after he became her soul mate. Then you were born, and they brought you with them. You were so tiny and beautiful.

On that night the portal opened, and we watched the three of you fly through. You each fluttered down to the ground, folded your wings and assumed your mortal forms. Denelia, Flora and I threw our arms around each other. We hugged and laughed together. Then Denelia asked us to keep you safe. She was going with Thistle to fight Villiana, and it was too dangerous to take you with them."

Aunt Janet continued telling the story. "We promised to protect you and keep you safe. Thistle placed strong protecting spells on you, the house, and the garden. He told me how to activate them after he and Denelia were gone. Those spells would block Villiana if she tried to enter the garden."

"My mother said I was to stay here with you," said Mary Alice, "but I didn't want to. I remember that she placed a ribbon with a golden key around my neck. "It will be invisible," she said. "It will be a link between you and me because it—"

The memory of that dark night now returned to Mary Alice's mind. She trembled as she remembered the whirlwind and the thick blackness that had twisted around them. Her mother's sentence was never finished. Mary Alice could not see anything and she had felt a horrible force clutch her and sweep her into the air. Aunt Janet pulled her back and held her close. She had felt safe, but she was frightened, too. Her heart beat rapidly and the noise from the whirlwind hurt her ears. Then the noise was gone. The twisting dark wind and her parents were gone.

The memory of that dark time left, but the tears that Mary Alice had shed when her parents left returned again. "Oh Aunt Janet, where are my parents? Why haven't they returned? I wanted to remember them. And now I do, but it makes me sad. I want them to come back."

Her aunt reached out and drew her close. Aunt Lillian wrapped her arms around them both.

"I love you, child," Aunt Janet murmured. "I promised your mother I would protect you and I will. Your magic is strong. It is stronger than I had ever imagined it might be. I did not truly want to take your magic away. We knew Villiana would look for a fairy child. So we thought the best protection was to have you be a mortal child."

It was a long while before Mary Alice went to bed. Both of her aunts slipped in to say good night. Many questions had been asked and answered that night. One memory after another had been shared as the time slipped quickly by. Now she lay in her bed, but sleep did not come easily.

She was thinking about her father, and she thought again about the thistle plant in the garden. *My father uses the thistle plant to send messages. So that thistle must know where my father is.* She felt that she simply had to talk to Thistle tonight. She listened intently. There were frogs singing in the garden. A cricket chirped outside the window. The house was silent. She slipped out of bed and tiptoed over to her bedroom door and cautiously turned the knob, opening the door just a little bit.

Aunt Lillian's voice said, "Don't go into the garden." Mary Alice peered up and down the hall, but she could not see her aunt anywhere. She opened the door a little wider, and heard Aunt Lillian say again, "Mary Alice, don't go into the garden." She looked down and saw a snowdrop blossom lying on the floor just outside her bedroom door.

"Drat," she said and carefully pulled the door shut.

She tiptoed over to the window. When she started to open it, she heard Aunt Janet's voice. "Mary Alice, do not go into the garden." A pink peony lay on the window ledge on the other side of the glass.

"Drat. Double drat," Mary Alice muttered as she returned to her bed.

A Bindweed Cage

Mary Alice was nestled in her bed. She couldn't go outside and she couldn't go to sleep. She had so much to think about. She smiled because now she had so many happy memories. However, she still wanted to know what had happened to her parents. She didn't remember everything that happened when that dark wind came. She had been frightened, and it was so dark that she didn't see what happened. *Nightshade knows. He said Thistle is trapped in a cage. Did he tell the truth? Or not? I wish I could see. . .* She abandoned all thoughts of sleep as she sat up in bed. *I can see. I have a spell I can use to see the past.* She became Maryalise and said the words of her spell.

Backward, turn backward
O time in thy flight.
Let me see Thistle
On that dark, dark night.

A misty curtain formed in front of Maryalise. When the mist drifted away, she saw her two mortal aunts in the garden. She watched the portal open and saw three tiny fairies fly into the garden. They landed on the ground and changed to mortal forms. Thistle, Denelia and Maryalise.

I'm here, and I can see me there. She was both nervous and excited as she anticipated what would happen next.

The dark twisting whirlwind swept into the garden, surrounding Maryalise and her family. Now that she was viewing those awful moments, she could see through the haze and she saw what happened to each member of her family.

The Maryalise from the past was snatched by an unseen force and sucked toward the center of that dark cloud. Aunt Janet wrapped her arms around the little girl, using the force of love and magic to pull her back and keep her safe.

Denelia changed to fairy form and started toward her daughter. The twisting wind sent her spiraling through the air and flung her through the portal. Then it closed.

Howling winds of darkness ambushed Thistle from behind while he was still in mortal form. Darkness twisted around him. He was caught in a thick, black snare. Although he struggled valiantly, he could not escape the evil force that held him fast. It was then that Thistle closed the portal. A frustrated screech tore through the garden, and Maryalise saw Thistle clap his hands over his ears. His body became limp, and the angry wind carried Thistle and the darkness away.

Now Maryalise (in her present form) felt as though she were being swept along inside that dark whirlwind with Thistle. The evil magic did not seem to sense that she had traveled with it.

When the darkness was gone, she saw that her father lay motionless on the floor of a large cavern. *Is he dead?* His hands and feet were shackled with iron chains. He opened his eyes, lifted his head, and his lips moved as he awkwardly waved his hands. He frowned and his hands stopped their motion. *He's trying to cast a spell, but it isn't working. Those chains must be powerful. They keep him from using his magic.*

The cavern was dark and it was hard to see. Greenish-yellow blobs on the walls and ceiling gave off a dim light. Many tunnels led into the cavern. Thistle lifted his head again as an icy wind blew across the cavern. A small black dragon flew into the cavern, landing beside him. Stepping down from its back, Villiana rose to mortal size. She was dressed in a flowing purple dress. Black hair curved around her cold but beautiful face, and her black wings glistened in the dim light.

"Thistle, you are my prisoner."

He remained silent.

"You are in my power," she sneered. Her eyes were black as obsidian daggers and she glared at her captive.

He still did not reply.

"Give me the secret of the portal!" demanded the Dark Fairy, "or I will destroy you and all that you love."

"No," Thistle said. "The secret of the portal will never be yours."

Villiana's hands curled into hard, angry fists. She leaned down and said, "I will obliterate your mate. I will take your child. She shall be mine."

Maryalise trembled. The dim cavern seemed to hold only darkness and despair. Fear swept into her heart. Her father was helpless, and everything seemed hopeless. He had no weapon. He had no way to fight. *But he won't give up. My father will never give up.*

The Dark Fairy's voice became softer as she wheedled, "Actually, I already have your child. Denelia gave her to me in exchange for her freedom." Villiana folded her arms across her chest and leaned closer to Thistle. "Denelia is free. I will let you join her and I will give your child back after you give me the secret of the portal."

She's lying. Maryalise tried to send her thoughts to her father. *Thistle, I am here—even if you can't see me. Can you hear my thoughts? She lies. I am safe. Aunt Janet is keeping me safe.*

She didn't know if her thoughts had reached him or not. But Villiana's cruel words lost power as Thistle gathered his courage to resist. He met the Dark Fairy's evil stare with calmness. "You lie," he said. "Denelia would die before giving our child to you. You do not have Denelia, and you do not have our child."

Maryalise clapped her hands silently. She did not want to reveal her presence. Villiana did not seem to know she was there. *That's right Thistle. Do not believe her. Do not let her win.*

Villiana's face twisted with fury. She stalked around Thistle and stopped once more to glare down at him. "I shall have them! I shall!"

Thistle did not speak.

Thistle doesn't believe her. Villiana doesn't understand the power of love. He will never give in.

Villiana snarled, "I will have the secret of the portal. Thistle, you are my prisoner. You are in my power, and you shall remain here forever unless you give me that secret." Reaching into the folds of her robe, she drew out a tiny object. She waved her hand in front of Thistle's face and held that misshapen seed up before his eyes. "You shall remain here," she snarled. "You shall remain here forever—unless. . ."

She did not need to finish her sentence. Her intentions were clear.

Villiana hurled the seed to the cavern floor. Slowly and deliberately she invoked her spell.

Seed of bindweed, twist and grow.
Send thy roots down deep below.
Let thy branches twist and twine,
Let thy tendrils and thy vine
Make a cage without a door.
Keep Thistle prisoner forevermore!

Maryalise heard a vicious, hideous laugh. The bindweed seed sprouted and began to grow. Three forked branches spread outward from the stem. Branches began to twist themselves together, and the top of the cage began to form. Villiana lifted her hands, palms upward, and she muttered another incantation.

Maryalise could not hear the words, but, as the evil fairy raised her hands, Thistle rose from the ground and was lifted up into the cage. The branches continued to twist and twine. Evil magic held him suspended as the vines constructed the bottom of the cage below him. When the cage was complete, Villiana abruptly turned her hands over and lowered them to her side. Thistle crashed to the bottom of the cage, and it swayed violently back and forth. He struggled to his feet. The chains clanked as he hobbled over to the edge of the cage. He attempted to push the branches apart, but it was no use. As fast as he broke one branch, another grew and twisted itself into place.

Villiana's laugh echoed through the cavern. "You can try," she taunted, "but you will find that there is no way out of this cage. And be assured that no one will be able to rescue you. I will make sure of that."

Villiana raised her fists high and cast another spell.

Cage for Thistle, made of tree,
A magic spell I cast on thee.
No leaf shall fall.
Nor vine untwine
'Til Thistle's secret shall be mine.
No spell can cut nor branches bend.
Never shall this magic end.

A wisp of dark gray smoke sprang from each upraised fist. Villiana uncoiled her hands and hurled the smoke forward. The smoke left her hands and flowed around the cage, one stream moving to the left and the other to the right. As they circled the cage, the tail behind each stream became longer and darker. The trails of smoke met on the far side of the cage, and streaks of darkness cascaded downward like a murky curtain, shrouding Maryalise's view.

Villiana's voice screeched in the darkness. "Thistle, remember. I will obliterate your mate. I shall have your child. I know where she is. She shall be mine!"

Maryalise trembled. She forgot that she was only an observer who could not be seen. "No!" she wailed. "Don't let her take me!"

The spell was broken. She was no longer Maryalise. She could not see Thistle. She had not found out where he was. She was back in her room. Mary Alice huddled on her bed and wept.

The Thistle Seed

Sleep was a long time coming. Mary Alice shivered. She felt the coldness squeeze her heart. She huddled under her blanket, wrapped her arms around her waist and moaned. *I wish I hadn't followed Thistle. No, I'm glad I followed Thistle. I wish I hadn't left him.* She muffled her sobs with the blanket. *I have to rescue him. I can't rescue him. I don't know where he is. Villiana wants me. Why? Why does she want me?*

Dark images twisted their way into her dreams. Bindweed laughed at her. He twisted his vine around her and yanked her into a smoky black cloud. She trembled and squeezed her eyes shut. She clapped her hands over her ears to shut out his hideous laugh. Then the roar stopped and she was no longer moving. She was laying on a bumpy surface. She listened carefully. *Someone is here. I can hear someone. But what is that clanking sound?*

She cautiously opened her eyes. She was Maryalise and in her fairy form. But that didn't seem to surprise her. She was inside the bindweed cage with her father. He was trying to free himself from the bindweed cage, but he could not break even the tiniest twig nor pluck a leaf from off a branch. The chains that bound his feet and wrists clanked as he beat against the vines. She flew up close to his ear and whispered, "Thistle, I'm here."

He did not answer. She reached out and touched his cheek, but she did not feel anything, and he did not respond. She wished she had her thinking cap. Maybe it could help her decide what to do. *I don't really need it*, she told herself as she organized her thoughts.

She wondered if she was dreaming or if she really was here with Thistle inside his cage. *He can't see me. He can't hear me either. But I see him. Am I a captive too?* Maryalise flew through the vines into the cavern and back inside again. *No, I'm not a prisoner. I must be dreaming.* She sat on one of the branches at the side of the cage. Apparently, there was a magical connection between them that had brought her back to Thistle. Once again she was an observer.

She watched Thistle hobble around the cage and she considered possibilities. *Will my magic work here? Do I dare use magic? Can I use magic in a dream? I wish I knew what Thistle was thinking.* Tiny sparkles drifted in the air between them. *Was that a magic spell?* She concentrated on the sparkles that connected her to her father. His thoughts began to travel to her. *I can hear what he is thinking. How did that happen?*

The darkness and despair in his heart was darker than the cavern. She continued to hear his thoughts. *I wish I knew how to escape. Where are Maryalise and Denelia? Are they safe?*

Maryalise felt his sadness. She knew that she was safe, but her father didn't. She flew over to land on his shoulder. "I'm here," she whispered in his ear.

Thistle did not respond. He could not hear her. She frowned and concentrated on what he was thinking. *I want to believe that they are safe in the Fairy Realm,* thought Thistle. *If they made it through the portal, they are safe because I locked it. No one but me can open it now. Perhaps they are safe in the garden with Flora and Annie*. He shook his head. *I don't think that Villiana has captured them—at least not yet. If they are in the garden. . . if Flora activated my protecting spells for the house and garden, then they are safe. Flora promised to protect Maryalise.*

His sadness was like a sharp knife that plunged into Maryalise's heart. *He is so sad and worried. If I can hear Thistle's thoughts, why can't he hear mine?*

She tried to think a message to her father. *I am safe. Denelia is in the Fairy Realm. We are safe.* When her father still did not respond, she knew he was not able to hear her thoughts. It saddened her to see his sorrow, but she could not bring herself to leave.

Time seemed to pass slowly. It was not possible to know whether it was day or night. The hours were filled with sorrow and fear. Shadowy creatures traversed the cavern from one tunnel to another. Although she could hear them hiss and snarl as they passed, she never could see them clearly. The light in the cavern was dim. They lurched across the cavern floor on short legs, stirring up clouds of dust that clung to their thick, dark, fur. Their bodies had a weird hump on their back. Sometimes she glimpsed ugly snouts, lashing tails, and sharp claws. Sometimes the fresh smell of earth followed a creature as it entered the cavern

Beasties with wings like bats, and angry monkey faces flew around the cage, smirking at Thistle with hideous grins. Sometimes they grabbed the branches of the cage with their hind legs and reached for him with their four front arms. Thistle remained in the center of the cage and their claws could not reach him. They snapped their tiny pointed teeth up and down and screamed at him. Although Maryalise believed the creatures could not see her, she flew to the center of the cage and huddled near Thistle.

Thistle rose to his feet. His chains clanked as he paced back and forth across the cage. He stopped near Maryalise and a small smile crept across his face.

Maryalise smiled, too. *He can't hear me, but I think he feels me near.* She watched as he shoved one hand deep into the pocket of his mortal clothes. When he pulled his hand out, it was curled tight. He opened his fist one finger at a time.

Maryalise flew up to see what he was holding. It was a thistle seed. Its fluffy parachute was still attached. A small breeze caused the seed to quiver in his hand. *Where did that breeze come from?* she thought. It smelled like warm earth and sunshine and flowers. Looking up, she saw a small hole in the roof of the cavern that she didn't remember seeing before. There was a flicker of movement. Thistle remained motionless for a long time and watched that opening.

Maryalise watched too. Two long ears appeared and then a head. *It's a rabbit. I think it's the one that lives in the garden. And if it is, then this cavern is under the garden.*

She watched the rabbit as it looked all around the cavern. *Go away, little rabbit. This is a dangerous place. Go away now before you fall in.* The rabbit pulled his head back and was gone. She wasn't sure whether he had understood her or was just tired of looking into the cavern.

Thistle lifted the seed high above his head and blew on it. He watched as it floated between the bindweed branches at the top of the cage. A gentle air current carried it higher. It floated above his head, spinning slowly, dipping this way and then that way.

I can help, thought Maryalise as she flew up. She wanted to guide the seed through the branches of the cage and up toward the rabbit's hole. She blew on it, but it did not change direction.

Drat. I wanted to help.

Thistle held his breath when the seed started to drift downward, but—at just that moment—a cold wind swirled into the cavern. The thistle seed's tiny parachute opened wider, and it floated up into the rabbit's hole and vanished from sight.

Villiana hovered near the cage. Thistle did not look around.

"Well," she demanded. "Are you tired of living in this cage? Have you come to your senses?" Her voice became softer, more compelling. "Thistle, have you thought of the power you might have? You and I, together we can rule time and space and dimensions. Give me the secret of the portal."

He closed his eyes and refused to answer.

My father knows that she must never have the secret of the portal. She is evil and must never enter the Fairy Realm.

His silence fueled her rage.

The icy wind left. She was gone, but her vengeful words echoed back into the cavern. "I am Villiana. You shall give me what I ask!"

Thistle looked for his seed. It was out of sight in the rabbit's hole. He smiled.

Maryalise's dream continued. She flew up through the rabbit's hole and found the spot where the thistle seed had drifted to the earth. She carefully patted the earth above the thistle seed. *So that's how the thistle got in the garden. It's Thistle's connection to us. The cavern is under the garden. He can send messages to us. Will he know when I'm dancing in the garden*? A tear trickled down her cheek. *But Denelia isn't here. She won't get any messages.*

The dream faded to nothingness and the dream connection to Thistle was gone. Mary Alice's cheeks felt wet.

The Birds

Mary Alice stretched and opened her eyes. The room was filled with light. The sun had already climbed high in the sky and she couldn't see it through her window. *That was some dream*. Just thinking about that nightmare made her shiver. *But it feels more real than a dream. Somehow I went back to be with Thistle. And now I know where he is.*

She expected to hear Aunt Janet or Aunt Lillian down in the kitchen, but the house was filled with silence. A row of birds was perched on the windowsill outside her bedroom. They were twittering a morning song. *Why are they there?* Mary Alice sat up in bed so she could see them better. They were looking in the window and seemed to be scolding her. She concentrated and the words of their song came into her mind.

It's time to get up, you sleepy head.
It's time to get out of your bed.
The day is a'wastin'.
You must be a'hastin'

"Oh, all right, all right!" said Mary Alice as she hopped out of bed. "Anyway, I want to go talk to Thistle." *I can talk to flowers. Now I'm talking to birds*. Her mind was full of questions to ask Thistle. *I wonder if my aunts slept this late, too.*

She opened her door slightly and peeked into the hall. Both of her aunts' doors were shut. The snowdrop blossom still lay in front of her door. Aunt Lillian's voice said, "Mary Alice, don't go out into the garden."

She giggled and then she whispered, "Snowdrop, its morning. Let me pass."

Snowdrop replied, "Mary Alice, don't go out into the garden."

She pulled the door shut and walked over to the window. The peony flower lay on the windowsill. It repeated the words it had spoken the night before. "Mary Alice, don't go into the garden." She nodded to the chorus line of small brown birds that were still perched on the windowsill. They sang louder.

The day's a'wastin'.
You must be a'hastin.'

One bird wasn't singing. It held a daisy in its tiny beak. Mary Alice opened the window, and it flew into the room. The heavy window slipped from her fingers and banged shut. *Oh, no. Did that wake my aunts?*

The bird circled her head and then flew down to drop the daisy into her hands. "Help Thistle," said Daisy. "Thistle needs you."

Mary Alice was frustrated. *Thistle needs me. But those flowers are telling me to stay in here. It's morning now. I wonder if Snowdrop or Peony will let me pass. What will they do if I try?* She concentrated—hard. *But I really do need to go outside Those flowers called me by name. They told Mary Alice, "Don't go out into the garden." But Mary Alice is a mortal child. Will they let someone who is not a mortal leave the room?* She lifted her arms and began to dance. Her white nightgown flowed as she twirled. She whispered,

I am Maryalise. Maryalise is me.
Not mortal, but a fairy will I be.

She became Maryalise and felt herself become smaller and smaller. Her nightgown became a glistening tunic. It was as delicate and airy as a cobweb—a rainbow of shimmering light. Her iridescent wings looked as if they had been embroidered with silken threads drawn from a rainbow. Her spell worked! She was in her fairy form. She fluttered her wings and rose into the air. She flew over to look at herself in the mirror. She had imagined being Maryalise before and knew that she had magic, but this was the first time she had actually changed to fairy form. Her laughter bubbled up and spilled into the air. She flew in circles around the room. *I'm flying. I'm flying. I didn't forget how! I didn't.*

The little brown bird had been perched on the foot of her bed. Now it took flight and headed for the window and the tiny fairy flew after it. The bird landed on the windowsill and pecked on the glass. "Oh, no!" wailed Maryalise. "I didn't prop the window up. We can't go out that way!"

Her feathered friend cocked its head to one side. It seemed to be waiting for Maryalise to find a way out of the room. She flew over to the door. It was shut, and there was only a thin crack under it. "We can't slip under the door," she told the little bird. "The crack is too small."

She balanced on the doorknob and considered possible solutions. Her tiny feet slipped, and she sat down abruptly. The doorknob wiggled. Maryalise stood up and bounced on the knob until the door swung slightly open. The fairy and the little bird flew through the crack and over the white snowdrop flower. It did not speak.

They winged their way down into the kitchen. The outside door was closed. A slight breeze touched her face and teased her hair. Aunt Janet had propped the kitchen window open a crack to let fresh air in. Maryalise landed on the windowsill, folded her wings, and crawled through the crack. "Follow me," she said.

The bird tried to follow, but the crack was too small. Its frantic chirping called her back.

"I'll come help you." She crawled under the window again and pushed on the little bird. Its beak bumped against the window frame. "Duck your head."

The bird lowered its head. Maryalise pushed harder. Tiny feet stuck out behind as the bird tobogganed on its tummy through the crack. When it reached the other side, it struggled to its feet and shook its ruffled feathers back into place.

Maryalise kept her wings close to her body and scooted through the crack again. "I knew we could do it," she said. The two of them stood together on the windowsill and waited until she had caught her breath. Then they flew across the garden toward the thistle plant. The rest of the flock flew from the windowsill outside her bedroom, moving into formation behind her.

Random thoughts drifted through her mind as she flew across the garden. *When I imagined I was a fairy, I thought I was pretending. But I wasn't.* The reason her pretending had seemed so real was probably because part of it was real. She wondered if she had remembered the flower names of Annie, Flora and Denelia and their chosen roles because of the stories her mother had told her.

Arriving at the thistle plant, Maryalise saw a dark cloud hovering above it. She flew toward that thick gray cloud and saw that it was made up of winged beasties. Like a swarm of angry mosquitoes, they circled the thistle blossom. They were the size of bats, and they had sharp pointed teeth. They snapped at the thistle plant and shreds of leaves flew through the air. There were so many of them that she could not see the thistle blossom. The stem of the plant shuddered.

"Stop that," she yelled.

They ignored her.

"Follow me," Maryalise cried to her winged flock. They circled in the air above the thistle and then dove down at the swarm. The flying beasties gathered themselves together in a tight ball and blocked Maryalise's path.

She tried to reverse her direction and tumbled head over feet in the air. The flying beasties swarmed toward her. Sharp teeth snapped at her. The flock of birds scattered. When Maryalise was able to regain control, she flew through the branches of the willow tree and landed on the ground beneath it. The winged beasties flew around the circle of stones but did not cross them. Maryalise could hear their nasty buzzing. The volume of the buzzing was less as they returned to the thistle plant and continued snapping at it.

She heard the birds chirp. "We're here." She looked up. They were perched above her head in the willow tree.

That was close. Her heart gradually slowed down. She settled herself on the ground and folded her wings. *I need a different plan. They're really mean.* Remembering the storm and the crystal, she wondered if she could call the light again. *I don't have a crystal today, but maybe magic will be enough.* After she had found the right words for her spell, she flew back out into the garden and hovered a safe distance away from the thistle plant before speaking.

Magic in me.
Magic in me.
Send sunshine gleaming,
Sunshine beaming.
Send a ray of sunshine down to me.
Make winged beasties fear and flee.

A ray of sunshine sliced through the thick, gray cloud and illuminated the thistle blossom. The flying beasties screeched angrily as they scattered and flew behind the garden shed. Maryalise flew after them, but when she got there, the beasties were gone.

"Thistle!" she called as she landed on a leaf of the thistle plant. She reached out and touched the blossom. "Are you all right?"

She didn't wait for a reply. She called out again, "Father, I am here."

"Hush," said Thistle. "There are spies in the garden. They will tell Villiana where you are."

Maryalise ignored Thistle's words. "I know where you are," she said. "I'll come and rescue you."

"No. It's too dangerous. Villiana's magic is strong. You must find the entrance to the cavern. Get Flora and Annie to help you seal it."

Maryalise shook her head. "I'll find the entrance. Then I'll come rescue you. I will. I am a fairy and I have magic."

"NO! Magic cannot save me. Find the entrance to the cavern. Get Flora and Annie to help you seal it. You must do that."

Maryalise fluttered into the air and began to look for the cavern entrance. *Where could it be?* Then she remembered the yucky feelings she always felt near the garden shed. *The entrance must be back there. That's where the beasties went.* She flew toward the back of the garden shed. The rotten smell was stronger now and she felt dizzy. *I'm not a quitter.* She flew back and forth and examined the area carefully, but she could not see the opening to the cavern. She landed in a bush, folded her wings and sat very still. *I will wait,* she decided. *They will probably come back.* The flock of small brown birds flew down and perched in the bush above her head.

She waited a long time and was about to give up when she saw a snout and then two fierce red eyes appear from a pile of sticks. *What is that?* Maryalise held her breath and remained motionless. Whatever it was looked all around. She saw one claw and then another claw emerge from the secret entrance. *It's one of those shadowy creatures from the cavern. I can't let it come into the garden.*

Maryalise whispered her spell.

> Ray of sunshine, bright you'll be.
> Ray of sunshine, fly with me!

Maryalise and the birds took flight. They flew directly at the beast's head. He snarled, shook his head and then vanished. When they arrived at the place where he had been, Maryalise landed on the ground. *Where did he go? He was here and then he wasn't. He went somewhere.* She studied the pile of sticks. She flew up and looked behind the pile. She flew back around and landed in the last place she had seen the creature. She picked up a twig and carefully poked it into the pile. The twig vanished. It reappeared when she pulled it back out.

"Very clever," she muttered. "It's an invisible curtain that pretends it's a pile of sticks. It must connect to the underground cavern where Thistle is." She considered going in—just far enough to see what the tunnel was like, but she changed her mind. *No, I won't. I need a plan. But I don't want any of those nasty creatures to come out again.* She focused her thoughts and cast a spell.

Ray of sunshine, oh so bright,
Guard this tunnel 'til the night.

There, she thought as she watched the ray appear. *Now they can't get out. They're afraid of light.* She was pleased with herself. *I must tell Thistle. I found the entrance.* She was bubbling with excitement as she landed on a thistle leaf, folded her wings, and reached out to touch the thistle blossom. Even though some of its petals were scattered across the ground, it seemed to be all right. The thistle blossom leaned toward Maryalise.

"Thistle, I found the entrance. It's hidden behind a curtain that looks like a pile of sticks. I'll make myself invisible and come rescue you."

"No. You mustn't. Listen to me. I gave you protection. A strong magic spell encircles you. It will overpower any attempt to take you out of the garden. The moment you leave the garden, your protection is gone."

"I will protect myself. I have magic."

"No. You're magic isn't strong enough. When you enter the tunnel, the evil ones will sense magic. They will seize you. I couldn't bear it if they captured you. Villiana's magic is powerful. You cannot rescue me with magic."

"My magic is strong," insisted Maryalise. "I will rescue you!" Her wings quivered. *I have to rescue him. I'll find a way.*

"Maryalise," said Thistle. "Go find Flora and Annie. Tell them to seal the entrance to the cavern."

"Yes, I'll talk to them." She slowly flew toward the house, and a deep sadness poured into her heart. *I am Thistle's daughter. I cannot bear to have him trapped forever in that cavern. I have to rescue him. There has to be a way.* She hovered in the air and looked back at the thistle blossom. *I have magic. And if I can out-stubborn Aunt Janet and Aunt Lillian, I can out-stubborn Villiana.*

She landed on the kitchen windowsill. She turned and waved at the flock of birds. "Thank you," she called. Then she crawled back through the crack. The tiny fairy flew up the stairs and into her room. She was sitting on the footboard of her bed thinking when she heard footsteps in the hall. Quickly she said:

I am Maryalise. Maryalise is me.
Not fairy, but Mary Alice will I be.

The change was complete before the door swung open, and Aunt Lillian stepped into the room. "Mary Alice," she said, "what are you doing perched up there on the end of your bed?" Aunt Lillian waved her finger at Mary Alice as she smiled and pretended to scold. "You are such a lazy child. The morning is half begun, and here you are still in your nightgown." Her aunt reached out and pushed Mary Alice. She laughed as she fell backward and landed on her bed. She bounced up and down.

Aunt Lillian stood with her hands on her hips. "Janet has breakfast ready, and she says to come eat before it gets cold. Hurry and get dressed, you lazy child."

Mary Alice smiled at Aunt Lillian. *She is pretending to scold, but she isn't really mad.* Mary Alice spread her arms wide on the bed and laughed again. *I need a rescue plan. I'll tell my Aunts about the entrance after I rescue Thistle.*

She looked up into her aunt's twinkling eyes. "I'll hurry. Tell Aunt Janet I'll be down for breakfast as soon as I get dressed."

The Rescue Plan

Mary Alice absently stirred her lumpy oatmeal as she thought about a rescue plan. She wasn't interested in eating or talking. "You haven't eaten your oatmeal," said Aunt Janet. "Are you feeling all right?"

Aunt Lillian got up from her chair, walked around the table, and placed her hand on Mary Alice's forehead. "No fever," she said. Aunt Lillian returned to her chair, but continued to observe her niece.

"I'm all right," Mary Alice insisted. "I'm just thinking." She forced herself to eat a few bites of oatmeal and then asked, "Can I go now?" She pushed her chair back from the table and stood up. When she started toward the door to the garden, she saw Aunt Lillian glance at Aunt Janet. Aunt Janet glanced back at Aunt Lillian. Aunt Lillian shook her head back and forth slightly. Although no words were spoken, Mary Alice had the feeling that a message had been passed from one aunt to the other. Aunt Janet spoke, "Have you made your bed and straightened your room yet?"

Mary Alice shook her head no. *My Aunts obviously don't want me to go out there.* Aunt Lillian stood up and went out the door to the garden. *I'll bet Aunt Lillian is checking to make sure it is safe*. Mary Alice trudged up the stairs. She hastily pulled the covers up on her bed, shoved her nightgown into a drawer, and hurried back down to the kitchen. She entered at the same time that Aunt Lillian came in from the garden. Aunt Janet turned from the sink, dishcloth in one hand, dirty plate in the other.

"My bed is made," said Mary Alice. "I'm going outside now."

Aunt Janet looked at Aunt Lillian, who nodded her head slightly. Then she looked back at Mary Alice. "Yes, child," she said, "you may go outside now."

Mary Alice ran out the door, down the steps and into the garden. She bent down and touched a pink daisy. "I'm trying to think of a rescue plan, Daisy. I need to rescue Thistle."

For a long moment, she thought that Daisy wasn't going to answer, but she did. "No magic. Magic won't work. Dangerous."

"Can you tell me anything about the tunnel and the cavern under the garden?"

Once more Daisy's answer was a long time coming. "Ask Dandelion. Dandelion's roots go deep. Ask Dandelion."

"Of course. Why didn't I think of that." There was a dandelion blooming in the middle of the daisies. She touched it and said, "Tell me about the tunnel and the cavern where Thistle is a prisoner."

"The tunnel is dark," said Dandelion. "It is protected by dark magic. Magic can't rescue Thistle."

"I know that! Everyone keeps telling me that I can't rescue Thistle with magic. I'm not going to use magic."

Dandelion ignored Mary Alice's outburst. "The tunnel is long and dark. Dark magic guards it. Magic will be detected in the tunnel. There is a large cavern. Thistle's cage is in the cavern."

"I know that! Tell me. How can I rescue him?"

"That I cannot tell you. I do not know. Do not go with magic."

"I won't," said Mary Alice. "I already said that I'm not going to use magic.'

"What did Thistle say?" asked Dandelion.

"I need to go." *Dandelion asks too many questions*, Mary Alice hurried on down the path. She parted the willow branches and entered her secret place. She sat down and concentrated. "The tunnel is dark. Thistle is in the cavern," she muttered. "Magic won't work. Nobody thinks I can rescue him, but I can. I have to." She concentrated harder. *I destroyed Nightshade without magic. Nightshade said that I was just a little girl. He thought I was a mortal child, but I destroyed him.* Her frown changed to a smile. *That's it. I can go down into the cavern as a mortal. I can't use magic so I will use mortal weapons.*

She slipped out from under the willow tree and ran to the garden shed. Aunt Lillian's snippers and a small garden shovel were hanging from hooks on the wall. She looked around to see what else might be useful. *Salt? Why are all those boxes of salt out here? And who put them here?* She answered her own question. *Aunt Lillian. She used salt to kill Bird Claw. She wants them here in case Bird Claw or other evil weeds come into the garden.* Mary Alice took four boxes of salt from the shelf. Aunt Lillian's gardening apron was hanging on a nail. Mary Alice loaded the salt, the snippers, and shovel into the apron's big pockets. After tying the apron strings together, she slung the improvised bag on her shoulder.

It's dark in the tunnel, she thought as she hurried back to the willow tree. *That's what Dandelion said. I can't use magic to see.* As she parted the branches and entered her secret place under the willow tree, she remembered her flashlight. *It's a mortal device.* She was glad that Aunt Lillian had helped her put a new bulb in it. Mary Alice set her apron-bag of tools down. *If I go to the house and get my flashlight, Aunt Janet might give me more chores. I don't have time for that. I need to rescue Thistle now.*

She remembered the day that she had summoned Annie's notebook. "That's it. I'll use my summoning spell!" She sat down and placed her hands in her lap with the palms upward.

Flashlight, oh flashlight,
Listen now, I summon thee.
From out of my room, from by my bed,
I command that you secretly come to me.

She closed her eyes and waited, pleased that she had thought to tell the flashlight to come secretly. There was a rustling sound—the sound of someone or something parting the willows. Her flashlight dropped into her hand. Curling her fingers around it, she opened her eyes. She smiled as she stuck the flashlight into her apron-bag. *I'm almost ready*. She lifted her hand, invoked the spell and the golden key appeared. She unlocked the chest and looked inside to see what else might be useful. *I might need that pocket knife*, she thought as she picked it up. *I wonder why Denelia kept a pocket knife in here*. She shrugged her shoulders and dropped it into the apron-bag. It clinked as it hit the shovel.

She wondered if she had thought of everything. She locked the chest and hid it again. She decided that she should probably leave a note for her aunts. *They'll probably worry anyway, but at least they'll know why I've gone*. She needed a pencil and paper. *No problem. I'll just summon them from my room*. After the pencil and paper arrived, she wrote a note.

Don't worry about me. I've found out where Thistle is, and I'm going to rescue him.

She couldn't think of anything else to say, so she signed it:

Love, Mary Alice.

If I leave the note here, Aunt Janet and Aunt Lillian might not see it. I think I should put it in my room. So she used a sending spell.

Little note, hear
What I've said.
Fly through the air.
Stop on my bed.

She watched as the note lifted into the air, dipped one side as if to say good-bye and floated away. It turned vertically and drifted between the branches of the willow tree. In her mind, she imagined it floating over the flowers, lifting up into the air, gliding through her window, and settling on her pillow. She grinned. *I'm Mary Alice. And I have a plan.*

Now I can go, as soon as I'm sure no magic is traveling with me. She smiled at her little joke, but—just to be sure—she said,

Magic stay inside this place
It's a mortal I must be.
Let no magic to me cling
Only a mortal can set Thistle free.

Mary Alice shouldered her apron-bag. She marched out of her secret place. She marched past the thistle. She marched past the flowers. She did not stop to talk. *I am a mortal right now and mortals do not talk to flowers*, she told herself. Her steps faltered as she approached the garden shed. *I can do this.* She took a deep breath and slowly let it out. *I have to do this.*

She stopped in front of the weed pile. A sunbeam shone down on the pile of sticks. *Sunbeam still guards the entrance.* However, she did not speak to the sunbeam *because mortals do not talk to sunbeams.* She looked at the pile of sticks. Even though she could not see it, she knew that the entrance was here. Fear crept into her mind and twisted around her heart. *If I stand here thinking, fear will twist itself around my legs, my feet will root themselves to the ground, and Thistle will be a captive forever.*

Mary Alice knelt down and gingerly poked her hand into the pile of sticks. She moved her hand from side to side and up and down. *Good. The entrance is big enough for me.* She poked her head through the hole. It was dark inside the tunnel. *Maybe this isn't a good idea. Maybe I should ask the aunts to come with me.* She shook her head back and forth. *No. I have magic I can do this*. Then she remembered that magic wouldn't work. *I have magic, but I'm not going to use it. I have to do this*. She forced her fears away and crawled into the tunnel. Then she stood up.

The tunnel was larger here. *Now what?* She took her flashlight out, but she didn't turn it on. She cautiously felt along the tunnel wall as she inched her way forward. The tunnel curved sharply. She stopped. *What was around there?* She reached into her apron-bag and grabbed the pocketknife. She tucked her flashlight under her chin while she opened it. She held the knife in her right hand and the flashlight in the other hand. *Should I turn my flashlight on now? Or wait?* She decided to wait.

She fingered the switch as she crept around the bend. *I don't need my flashlight*, she realized. The yellow-green things that were sticking to the walls and ceiling glowed. They looked like gigantic blobs of jelly. But they smelled like rotten eggs. The light was dim, but she could see. However, just in case, she kept her finger on the switch of her flashlight. She stood still to let her eyes adjust to the dim light, and she felt something twist itself around her feet and legs.

"Whooo are you?" hissed a voice from the shadowy gloom. "What isss the passssword?"

Glancing down, she saw that tendrils of some awful weed were wrapping themselves around her feet and her legs. They were twisting their way upwards.

"I am a mortal. I don't need a password." She stabbed and cut each tendril with her pocket knife. When her legs and feet were free, she looked down at the writhing pieces of weed. She watched two pieces join together again. "I know what to do with you. You can have some of Aunt Lillian's salt." Mary Alice put her knife and flashlight into the apron-bag and grabbed a box of salt. She emptied it on the pieces of weed and watched them turn brittle and black.

She shuddered and stepped over the pile of blackened remains. *I don't have time to dig out the roots. But I won't be here when it grows again—at least I hope I won't be.* She dropped the empty salt box and pushed that thought away.

Arming herself once more with her knife and flashlight, she inched her way on down the tunnel. She crept around the next bend and felt something soft and slimy push against her from each side of the tunnel. Two huge shapeless blobs were squeezing her and the rotten egg smell was much stronger now. These blobs were much larger than the ones on the walls and ceiling. She looked up and saw that the gooey blobs on the ceiling were squishing themselves together. They were slithering and sliding toward her.

At first, the creatures did not appear to have an obvious face. Mary Alice watched as one cold blue eye after another opened. Each blob had lots and lots of eyes and every eye was staring right at her. Looking away from the slimy blobs that were forming and advancing towards her, she concentrated on the two that held her prisoner. She used her knife to stab one of the creatures. When she pulled her knife out, the hole vanished. She stabbed again, slicing one blob in half. The two pieces simply rejoined each other and moved back into place to block her path.

"Leave me alone," she cried. "Go away! I want to go past!"

The creatures did not answer but pressed closer. She could not move forward. Her hands shook and her knees quivered. She stared back at all those cold blue eyes. *Maybe I should go back. Or maybe I could use a magic spell to destroy the blobs.* She tried frantically to think of a magic spell, and she remembered. *I am a mortal. Mortals do not have magic. Can I go back? Maybe I should.*

She wiggled and found that she could move slightly backward. *Dandelion warned me. Thistle told me not to come. But I have to rescue him.* Thinking about rescuing Thistle strengthened her and gave her power. *I can do this. I have to do this.* She turned on her flashlight and looked for a way to escape. When the beam of light hit the eye of an advancing blob, it moaned. Then it slowly melted like ice and became a puddle on the floor.

"So," Mary Alice muttered as she directed her light into the eyes of one creature after another. "You don't like light. Well, I do."

After she had melted all the creatures, she looked down at her feet. She was standing in a large pool of yellow-green slime. It jiggled back and forth as if it were trying to reform itself. She put her knife away, tucked her flashlight under her chin, and pulled out her second box of salt. When she sprinkled the salt on the pool of slime, it began to shrivel. It turned deep purple and then darkened to black. There was a tiny moan as the last of the black slime settled heavily on the tunnel floor like a layer of stinky dried mud. She dropped the empty box.

This part of the tunnel was darker now. The only light came from her flashlight. *Shall I turn it off? If I do, any other creatures that might be lurking in the tunnel won't see me, but I won't see them either. I think I'll keep it on.* Mary Alice cautiously moved forward, keeping the light from her flashlight low to the ground. Seeing the light push the darkness away was very reassuring.

The tunnel curved again. Keeping close to the wall, she inched around the bend and found that she was at the entrance to a large cavern. She warily swept the beam of her flashlight across the darkness. There were many tunnels that connected to this cavern. She didn't see any nasty creatures, but she knew they were probably here—somewhere. She directed her beam to the center of the cavern.

A thick stem rose from the floor of the cavern. Three large branches spread out from the stem and bindweed vines twisted in and out and around to form a cage that was suspended in the air. She started forward. *Thistle's cage. I've found him.* She stopped herself. *I must be careful. Haste makes waste. That's what Aunt Lillian says. I need to know what is out there. I need to know my way back.*

She tried to memorize what her tunnel looked like, but they all looked the same. She gathered several rocks and piled them against the wall. She scratched a mark on the wall with her pocket knife. The beam from her flashlight made a slow sweep around the cavern, pausing at each tunnel that entered it. When she was sure it was safe, she crept into the cavern and stood below the cage. Directing the beam of light through the vines, she saw Thistle. He was trapped in his mortal form inside that cage of twisted bindweed. It did not have a door.

I have found him.

"Thistle," she whispered. "I am here. I have come to rescue you."

The Cavern

In the shadowy darkness, Mary Alice could see Thistle sitting in the center of that twisted bindweed cage. His head was hidden in his hands. When he heard her voice he raised his head, and an expression of joy flashed across his face. It was instantly replaced by a wave of fear.

"Maryalise! What are you doing here? Go back. Quick!" he said, "Before they know you are here."

No!" She stamped her foot. "Not until I rescue you."

"Maryalise," pleaded Thistle, "Listen to me. They will sense your magic."

In spite of the intensity of the moment, her fear slipped away. "I'm not a fairy today. I have no magic. Today I am just Mary Alice. I am a mortal, and I have come without magic to rescue you." She looked up at Thistle. "Why do you stay in this cage? You could change into your fairy form and fly away."

Thistle lifted his hands. The iron bands on his wrists and ankles were connected by long chains. They clanked as he shook his hands. He said, "These chains are made of iron. They prevent me from using my magic to escape. I was trapped as a mortal, and now I cannot change to fairy form."

Mary Alice nodded her head. "Then it's a good thing I came. First thing is to get you out of that cage." After placing her flashlight on the ground, she put her knife back in the apron-bag and took the snippers out. She stood on tiptoe and tried to cut the bindweed vines on the bottom of the cage. Even though she squeezed the snippers as hard as she could, she could not cut even the tiniest vine. She could not cut a leaf. "This is powerful magic."

"That's what I told you," said Thistle. "I am imprisoned by magic and magic cannot save me."

Despair crept into her mind. If he was imprisoned by magic, how could she rescue him without magic? She remembered Aunt Lillian killing Bird Claw with mortal weapons, and she remembered destroying Nightshade without magic. *I can do this. There has to be a way to get him out of this cage*, she told herself. Thistle's despair drifted down to her and threatened to smash her thoughts.

She closed her mind to all negative emotions and silently concentrated on the bindweed cage. She remembered that when she had traveled back in time she had seen the bindweed cage form around Thistle. She remembered seeing Villiana hurl the seed to the ground. The bindweed plant grew and wove itself into the cage around Thistle. Then Villiana cast a spell on the cage so it could not be opened, and the vines could not be cut.

A smile spread across Mary Alice's face. "She put the spell on the cage—not the roots. I think I know how to get you out." Dropping the snippers, she took the gardening shovel out of the apron-bag. She began to dig by the roots of the bindweed plant. Bindweed shook himself. It was as if he was waking from a deep sleep. "What are you doing, Mortal?"

She ignored him and continued digging. Thistle knelt on the cage floor and watched.

"You cannot dig me up. My roots go deep."

"Don't listen to him," Thistle said.

Mary Alice did not answer Bindweed. *I am a mortal. I do not talk to plants.* The ground was hard, but she continued digging until the top of the taproot was exposed. *I hope this is deep enough.*

Bindweed swayed back and forth, causing the cage to swing above her head. "I am too strong. I am too powerful for you."

"We shall see," she muttered. She laid her shovel down and took out her pocket knife. Mary Alice slashed the roots until they had many nicks and cuts in them.

Bindweed's taunting laughter echoed through the cavern. "Those tiny cuts can't hurt me."

She reached into her apron-bag and took out her third box of salt. Doubts crept into her mind. *What if this doesn't work? What will I do when the salt is all gone?* She pushed those thoughts away and carefully poured salt on the nicks in the root and into the hole she had dug. Bindweed began to tremble and the cage shook. Its vines turned a deep purple as they began to untwist, and the leaves shuddered as they dropped to the cavern floor. The cage sank lower. The vines on the bottom of the cage snapped. Bindweed shrieked an unearthly cry of rage. Thistle plunged to the cavern floor. He struggled to his feet.

Mary Alice threw the empty salt box down and hugged her father. Tears of fear and joy spilled out of her eyes and slid down her cheeks. "I did it," she sobbed. "You are free."

Thistle hugged his daughter. The chains felt hard against her. He said, "Now go. Villiana's creatures will come. They will have heard Bindweed's cry."

She tugged on her father's hands. "Come. Let's go!"

"You must go without me," said Thistle. "These chains will slow me down. I will follow as fast as I can."

"No. I won't leave you. I'll help you." She picked up her flashlight and began to look for her pile of rocks and the mark on the tunnel wall.

They heard the shuffling noise of feet and a low rumbling. Mary Alice looked and saw shadowy creatures lurching into the cavern. The creatures surrounded them. The circle grew smaller and tighter.

Mary Alice thrust the flashlight into Thistle's hand and pulled out her last box of salt. She spread a circle of salt around Thistle and herself, concentrating intently to make sure there was not even the tiniest break in the circle. She huddled by Thistle's side. The creatures crowded closer.

She held her breath when the creatures reached the circle of salt and smiled when they could not cross it. They snarled and growled as they lurched around the circle, seeking a way in. Their shrieks of rage were music to her ears. In the dark murky clouds of dust that clung to the rough fur of the creatures, she caught glimpses of ugly snouts, sharp teeth, vicious claws, and lashing tails. The creatures snarled louder and louder. She trembled.

Thistle said, "Their cries will bring the flying beasties. They can fly over the salt circle. Villiana will come, too. Change into your fairy form and fly away."

Mary Alice knew that her father was right. She was only a mortal, and she feared that a mortal could not fight evil such as this. She spoke the words of her spell.

I am Maryalise.
Maryalise is me.
Not mortal,
But a fairy will I be.

She became smaller and lighter. Maryalise unfolded her wings and fluttered into the air. She looked down at Thistle. *I can't leave Thistle here. I want to take him with me. Thistle can't use his magic, but I can use mine.* She hastily devised a spell.

This is Thistle.
Thistle is he.
Not mortal,
But a fairy he must be.

Thistle began to change from mortal to fairy. He diminished in size, and his tiny hands and feet slipped free of the chains. He reached out, grasped Maryalise's hand and unfolded his wings. They rose into the air. The flying beasties circled in the cavern. Every exit was blocked and the beasties were getting closer. Maryalise could hear their sharp teeth snapping. The creatures below continued to snarl.

"This way!" said Thistle and he pulled her up toward the roof of the cavern. He waved his hand and particles of dust rose from the cavern floor and whirled around the two fairies. They flew up through that dust and into the small rabbit hole. Thistle stilled his wings and put a finger to Maryalise's lips. She nodded to let him know she understood. There must be no sound to reveal their hiding place behind the curtain of dust.

They listened to the frustrated whine of flying beasties. Maryalise sensed Villiana's presence in the cavern before she heard her speak.

"You idiots! She came into my cavern and you didn't see her! You let them escape. Find them!"

The buzz of the flying beasties diminished and then vanished as they flew into the tunnels, fleeing from the wrath of Villiana. Her voice rose from the cavern floor. Her rage now seemed to be targeted at the shadowy things upon the ground. "Stupid creatures! I sent you into that garden. You said that there was no fairy child there. Did your dense brains ever think to tell me that there was a mortal child in the garden?"

The dust began to settle and Maryalise watched the shadowy things cringe away from Villiana, snouts and tails pulled back inside the murky shadows that hid their bodies. One of them poked his snout out and emitted a series of squeaks and squeals. A bolt of power shot from Villiana's finger and the creature dissolved. Only a pile of dirt remained. "There was magic in that garden and you did not think to tell me!" she screeched. Each shadowy thing backed into the nearest tunnel and scurried away.

The dust had settled now. Maryalise stared down at the dark fairy. Villiana raised her fist. Thistle grabbed his daughter's hand and the two fairies flew up into the garden to land beside the rabbit's hole. A bolt of black lightning followed them and shot past them into the air.

Maryalise held her breath and trembled as she stared at the rabbit's hole. Nothing else happened. "Will she follow us?"

Thistle shook his head. "No. I don't think so. At least not right away. The protecting spell on the garden would weaken her power. She has been locked out. And she knows we would be watching for her."

Maryalise smiled.

"But she won't give up," Thistle said. "She will find a way."

They hovered above the rabbit's hole. Villiana's spies had not been stopped by the protection spell. Maryalise knew that if the flying beasties discovered this hole, they would swarm into the garden. Those creatures must be trapped in the cavern. "If it worked once, it will work again," she said as she prepared to invoke her spell.

Ray of sunshine,
Oh so bright,
Guard this hole
Against creatures of the night.

She hovered in the air and watched a ray of sunshine position itself above the rabbit hole. "I like that spell. But we'll need a new one when it gets dark."

"I like it, too!" said Thistle, echoing her words. "It's a good spell. I'm proud of you." He drew her close and hugged her. Then he pulled away. "Quick! Where is the entrance into the cavern? We must place a guard there also."

"It's already there. Let's go tell the aunts that you are rescued."

They flew over the flowers, across the garden, and into the house. The aunts were sitting at the kitchen table. Winged dandelion messengers covered the table. Aunt Janet's head was buried in her arms and Aunt Lillian was dabbing the tears away from her own eyes. "Mary Alice is in danger," Aunt Janet was sobbing, "and we don't know where she is or how to help her."

"Here I am!" Maryalise cried out. "I'm back and I have rescued Thistle!"

She landed in the middle of the winged messengers and sent them flying. They began to repeat their messages:

"Can't find Thistle."

"is in danger."

"Open portal."

"I sense my child"

"Must help her."

The winged messengers floated toward the ceiling. Thistle and Maryalise flew to catch them and return them to the table. "They are messages from Denelia," said Thistle as they laid the winged messengers back on the table.

The messengers arranged themselves in their proper order and gave their messages once more. "Can't find Thistle. I sense my child is in danger. Open portal. Must help her."

Maryalise looked at her aunts. "She's in the Fairy Realm. Open the portal. Denelia is waiting there."

Aunt Janet looked up. Her expression flickered from sorrow to joy and back to sorrow. "We can't," she said. "The spell we devised to open the portal requires three, and we are only two."

"Thistle," Aunt Lillian said, "you are the guardian of the portal. You can open it."

"Yes," he said. "I am the guardian. The Fairy Queen granted that power to me for as long as I live. When Denelia and I brought Maryalise through the portal, there was already an automatic lock in place. So the portal could only be opened from inside the Fairy Realm. I managed to shut the portal when I was captured. I couldn't let Villiana have access to the Fairy Realm. Now the portal can only be unlocked from the other side."

"Then Denelia can unlock it!" cried Maryalise.

Thistle eyes looked sad as he slowly shook his head back and forth. "No. Only I can unlock it."

"Then make another portal. Open a different portal." Maryalise stared at her father.

"I want to. But I can't. All portals into the mortal world are locked from the inside."

"We can't leave Denelia trapped in the Fairy Realm." Maryalise fluttered her wings rapidly. "There has to be something you can do. I want my mother. Here. Now." But she knew that all the wanting wouldn't open the portal.

She stomped her foot. The winged messengers took flight again, but no one tried to recapture them. She jammed her fists on her hips and glared at her father. "If you can't find a way, then I will."

She turned to Aunt Janet. "I know that you thought of a magic spell. You opened the portal once. You can do it again!"

Aunt Janet shook her head back and forth once more. Her voice was soft and gentle. "That spell required all three of us together. Now we are two. Our magic was never as strong as Denelia's. After she was gone our magic got weaker and weaker."

Aunt Lillian said, "It was only after you came that it began to get strong again."

Maryalise scrunched her eyebrows down and her nose upward as she tried to think. "I know how we can open the portal. Aunt Janet couldn't put a forget spell on me so she cast a spell that gave everything that was Denelia's to me." Maryalise laughed.

Aunt Janet looked puzzled. Aunt Lillian smiled and nodded.

"First, I need to be in my mortal form." She waved her hands and spoke her spell.

I am Maryalise.
Maryalise is me.
Not fairy,
But a mortal will I be.

Her wings folded, and she grew larger as she assumed her mortal form. She was standing on the kitchen table and she looked down into Aunt Janet's startled eyes. "Sorry," she mumbled as she scrambled off the table. She grabbed her aunts' hands and pulled them out into the garden. "All that is Denelia's is mine. Everything! I can take her place and we can open the portal."

Her aunts looked doubtful, but they followed Mary Alice. The three stood together in the center of the garden. They clasped their hands to make a circle of unity. Thistle hovered in the air and watched. Mary Alice said, "I stand here in Denelia's place. You are Flora and Annie. Say the spell with me. You remember the words?" Annie and Flora nodded their heads. Together they said,

We are three—the power of three.
Together we call on the powers that be.
Open the portal—open it wide,
Doorway to dimensions on the other side.
We are three—the power of three.
Together we call on the powers that be.

Mary Alice watched the portal open. First, she saw the tiny circle of light that got bigger and brighter. Misty golden light poured through the portal from the Fairy Realm and into the garden. The mist cleared. Mary Alice smiled when she saw Denelia fly into the garden. Thistle flew to meet her. They clasped hands, and they twirled and danced in the air. Mary Alice quickly changed to her fairy form and joined them in their dance.

After the Rescue

Maryalise twirled and danced with her parents, and it seemed as if all the flowers in the garden were singing in harmony. The air was filled with rainbows and sunbeams and music. She looked down at her aunts. Radiant light flooded the garden and surrounded them, too. They seemed to be a part of the melody and the dance even though their voices were silent and their feet remained planted upon the ground. *But*, she remembered, *they aren't Aunt Lillian and Aunt Janet—they're Annie and Flora.*

She fluttered down and gently landed on Aunt Lillian's shoulder. "We did it," she said as she folded her wings. "We did it together. We opened the portal, and now Denelia is back."

Aunt Janet looked at Maryalise and smiled. Her voice sounded softer, younger. "You did it. We needed the strength of your magic to open the portal and bring Denelia home."

Thistle and Denelia drifted down to the ground and assumed their mortal size. Aunt Lillian threw her arms around Denelia, causing Maryalise to tumble off. She spiraled—head over wings—almost to the ground. The falling sensation frightened her for a moment. Then she fluttered her wings and turned herself right side up. Her feet grazed the ground, but her wings carried her upward.

Aunt Lillian didn't notice Maryalise tumble, but Aunt Janet did. With outstretched hands, she attempted to catch the small fairy. She smiled as Maryalise rose into the air. "Are you all right, child?" she called.

"I'm all right," Maryalise replied as she hovered in front of her aunt. She drifted down to the ground and changed to mortal form. *It's easy*, she thought as she grew larger, *to change myself back and forth. I don't even need my spell anymore. I just think about changing and it's done.*

Mary Alice watched the three sisters. They smiled and laughed. A glimmer of tears sparkled in their eyes. Everyone hugged everyone else over and over again. There was so much to talk about, and Mary Alice wanted to share it all. She wanted to hear every word, but she had so much energy and joy inside that she couldn't contain her exuberance.

She changed to fairy form once more and flew above the garden doing acrobatics in the air. She plucked a leaf from the willow tree. Throwing herself down on it, she grabbed the stem with both hands and tobogganed down the gentle breeze. As the leaf touched the ground, she changed to mortal form and stood beside Denelia again. Everyone was talking at once.

"When that dark whirlwind came," Denelia was saying, "it sucked Thistle into it. Just as I changed to fairy form, the twisting wind threw me through the portal." Denelia looked at Mary Alice. "I turned to come back. I saw Flora holding you. Then the portal closed. Thistle was gone and I couldn't get to you. I tried to open the portal, but his magic lock was too strong."

Mary Alice interrupted, "But there are other portals. Why didn't you come back through one of them?"

Denelia looked into Mary Alice's eyes. "I tried, but Thistle had locked them all. He's Guardian of the Portals, and he was determined to keep Villiana out of the Fairy Realm. I couldn't find a way to return to the garden. I wasn't sure that I would ever be able to return. I knew that my sisters would keep you safe, but I wanted to be here too. I was so worried about you."

"It was a long time before I managed to send messengers," said Thistle. I was afraid Villiana's creatures would find her."

"But they couldn't find me, could they?" laughed Mary Alice. "I was here, disguised as a mortal child. I didn't even know I was a fairy because Aunt Janet transferred the Fairy Queen's Forget spell to me. And Villiana couldn't find me. She sent spies into the garden, and they didn't find me."

"I saw the thistle plant," Aunt Janet told Thistle.

"It grew right there beside the rabbit hole," said Mary Alice. "One day it wasn't there and the next it was. I talked to the thistle blossom. That's how I found out where you were, and I decided to rescue you."

"I told her not to come," Thistle told Denelia, "but she didn't listen. She came down into the cavern—without magic—and she rescued me. She was so very brave and resourceful."

Mary Alice was ready to burst with joy and happiness. Now that it was over and she didn't have to be scared, the rescue was an exciting story that she wanted to share.

While they were talking, the afternoon sun slipped lower in the sky. The sun blazed an orange-gold path as it descended toward the hills. Golden clouds wreathed the garden. Two rays of sunshine shone down into the garden with steady beams.

Suddenly Mary Alice remembered something that was more important than telling her story. "The cavern entrance. Thistle, we have to seal the entrance to the cavern. When it gets dark, the rays of sunshine will be gone. We can't let those evil creatures get back into the garden."

"I know," said Thistle. "We could seal the entrance and lock Villiana's creatures inside. But it is Villiana that we must conquer. The time has come to stop her. So we won't seal the entrance just yet. We'll wait, and she will bring the battle to us."

"Thistle," said Aunt Lillian. "Open the portal again. Send Mary Alice to safety. She is only a little girl."

"No!" said Mary Alice. "I want to help! This fight is my fight too."

Thistle looked down at Mary Alice and smiled. "I am counting on your help, daughter." He lifted his head and looked at Aunt Lillian. "No," he said gently, "We closed the portal after Denelia came through. It must remain closed. Never again can we let Villiana have access to the Fairy Realm. We will fight Villiana here and now with the magic we have. Maryalise's strong magic will be needed. We will fight Villiana and her evil minions with light and truth, and we will win!"

Fighting with Light and Truth

Thistle, Denelia, and Maryalise stood together on a broad leaf at the top of the thistle plant near the willow tree. It was taller than it had been before. The three fairies looked at Aunt Lillian and Aunt Janet who stood in the center of the garden. They had done all they could to prepare, and now there was just the waiting to endure. Maryalise looked at the dome of protection above the house and garden. Now that she had learned about Thistle's magic spell of protection, she could see the threads of magic shimmering in the sunlight if she looked carefully. Her eyes detected a wavering in one tiny area.

"Look, Thistle." She pointed to a place where the threads were starting to unravel. "The threads of the dome are thinner over there. We need to fix it."

Thistle nodded. "I see that weakness, too, but I want to see Villiana when she comes. She will see that weakness in the magic dome. Or she may come from the cavern. We will watch both places."

Maryalise nodded. She understood that it would be better to face the danger than to have it slip in behind them.

Long shadows stretched across the garden. The two rays of sunlight still guarded the pile of sticks and the rabbit's hole. Villiana's creatures were trapped in the cavern until the sun went down. The garden was silent. There was not even a breeze to sway the flowers or rustle the leaves.

A black cloud drifted across the sky toward the garden. Maryalise stared at that dark cloud. *Was it really a cloud? Or something else?* A cold wind swept into the garden and thick darkness pushed through the weak threads of the dome and rushed into the garden. A black dragon emerged from the darkness. Its massive wings beat up and down. Angry red eyes glared at the three fairies. A regal figure of mortal size balanced easily upon its back. Black hair swirled in the wind. Her purple dress streamed behind her. Widespread wings, dark and glittering, created a backdrop for her cold, merciless beauty.

"Villiana," whispered Thistle.

Maryalise wondered, *How could someone so evil be so beautiful?*

The dragon hovered in the air as the Dark Fairy diminished in size, gathering power into herself. Maryalise swallowed hard.

Thistle placed his hand on Maryalise's shoulder. "Be careful. She is more dangerous now."

Maryalise nodded. *I know. Maintaining mortal size dilutes a fairy's power.* She could feel the force of evil magic grow stronger.

Villiana stood on the dragon's head. She looked at Maryalise and called to her in a soft voice "Maryalise, my beloved child. At long last, I have found you."

What? I don't understand. How does she know my fairy name? She remained silent.

"My child, Thistle stole you from me. He wanted to steal your magic and make it his own. I needed the secret of the portal to rescue you." The Dark Fairy's hands reached out as she pleaded. "Come to me, my child. You will be a princess in a magical domain. We will be together again."

Maryalise remained motionless. A powerful force seemed to connect her to that magnificent fairy. *Could this be true?*

The Dark Fairy spoke again. "Come, my child. I love you. Thistle is not your father. He has blinded you with his lies. He does not love you."

Maryalise felt two strong hands upon her shoulders. There was love in that simple gesture, and she felt it warm her heart. "Remember that I love you," Thistle had said as they prepared for battle. "I believe in you. Together we will fight Villiana and her evil magic. Together we will win."

Thistle's daughter stood a little taller, threw her shoulders back, and stared directly into Villiana's eyes. "You lie. Thistle loves me. He is my father."

Villiana's beauty vanished. Her face twisted with rage and it became cruel and hard. Her vicious screams ripped across the sky. Clouds of darkness poured forth from the dragon's nostrils and coiled beneath the Dark Fairy before churning outward. Waterfalls of darkness fell upon the garden. Maryalise could feel the darkness gather around her. The sky was storm dark. The two rays of sunshine flickered and then vanished.

Villiana lifted her hands toward the sky as she summoned her creatures. "Come forth all ye creatures of darkness. Come forth. Destroy."

Hordes of darkness, like smoldering smoke, swarmed out of the tunnel and into the garden. The swarm of flying beasties circled above. Countless shadowy things scrambled across the ground, tails lashing, red eyes glinting, snouts poking out from the sinister dust clouds that cloaked their bodies from view.

Villiana threw her head back and laughed triumphantly. "Thistle, I shall have your child, and I shall have the secret of the portal." Standing upon the dragon's head, she raised one hand as though it held an invisible dagger. She muttered an incantation, and a black lightning bolt targeted Thistle.

He raised his hand. A gleaming ray of light emerged and a white lightning bolt surged into the air. Black lightning and white lightning collided. Fragments of black light and white light sparked in the sky. They exploded, fizzled and then were gone.

Yes, thought Maryalise, *Thistle's magic is strong.*

Villiana's rage boiled higher. Black lightning was thrust forward again, and again, to be met by Thistle's white lightning. The cycle of dark and light went on and on.

The Dragon seemed oblivious to the chaos above and around him as he hovered in the air. His malevolent eyes glared at Denelia. His stomach glowed fiery red as he built up heat. The dragon belched a fiery flame and sent it toward Denelia. She stretched her arms forward with her palms toward the dragon. Maryalise gasped and folded her wings against her body as the sizzling hot flame split and flowed around them. Denelia lifted one hand, summoning the water from the garden stream. Maryalise watched the water leave its bed and rise to quench the dragon's flame. The flame sizzled and vanished. A thick cloud of steam obscured Villiana and the dragon from view.

Maryalise watched Thistle throw yet another bolt of white lightning. *I can do that.* She stretched out her hand and called,

Bolt of lightning, come to me…

Maryalise couldn't think of a rhyming word. The spell fizzled and nothing happened.

Light of power, hear my call.
Bring to me a fireball.

That's a terrible spell. She was startled when a small ball of fire appeared in her hand. *I can't complain if it works.* "Take this, you evil things," she muttered, raising her hand. She intended to cast the fireball down into the middle of the creatures on the ground, but the fireball slipped from her fingers and spiraled through the air where it exploded. Two of the flying beasties screeched as they became balls of fire and then vanished.

She summoned a new fireball and searched for another target.

Aunt Janet and Aunt Lillian were fighting on the ground. Menacing shadowy creatures and flying beasties advanced toward them. Maryalise watched new bittersweet nightshade plants emerge from the ground, sending vines snaking across the garden toward the two mortals. *Aunt Janet promised to protect me. Tonight I will protect her.*

Her aunts had armed themselves with mortal weapons. "Our magic is too weak and our thinking too slow for rapid spells," they had explained, "so we will fight with what we have."

Nightshade vines snaked across the garden, weaving back and forth as they attempted to twist themselves around Aunt Lillian's arms and legs. She had armed herself with garden snippers. Her garden cart was loaded with every box and bag of salt from the garden shed and from the pantry. Zigzagging back and forth, she snipped the vines and poured salt upon the pieces. The nightshade plants twisted and writhed. They screamed in agony, turning black and brittle. Then they ceased moving.

Aunt Janet had armed herself with a flashlight and a large frying pan. The sharp pointed teeth of the flying beasties snapped, and they howled with malicious glee as they swarmed toward Aunt Janet. She gritted her teeth and flashed light into their eyes. Their cries of triumph became howls of rage and pain. They tumbled in the air and fell to the ground where she waited to flatten them and dead them forevermore.

Maryalise saw the hordes of creatures advancing toward her aunts. Snarling and clawing, with tails lashing, they retreated when the beam from Aunt Janet's flashlight hit their eyes. Maryalise laughed. *They're afraid of light. I'll give them some more.*

She took careful aim and threw her fireball into the middle of the creatures. Bright red sparks illuminated the garden. She grinned when she heard their squeals and saw them pull back, leaving fallen creatures behind. *I can do this*. She summoned and threw ball after ball of fire. Her arm got tired, but she refused to stop. She had killed a lot of them, but more and more creatures were coming out of the cavern. *How many are there? How can we fight them all? How can we ever win?*

Fear crept into her mind and twisted into her heart. The battle raged on and on. *Villiana is so powerful.* Her confidence wavered. She watched Thistle cast lightning bolt after lightning bolt. She watched Denelia summon water from the stream, quenching the dragon's flame each time it blasted forth. *I don't have that kind of magic.*

It was at that moment that Thistle glanced down at Maryalise and smiled approvingly. *I'm helping some*, she told herself. *I'm doing what I can.*

The winged beasties buzzed around Aunt Janet's head, their hideous faces contorted with glee, their knife-sharp teeth slashing at her arms and face. Maryalise raised her arm to hurl a fireball at the swarm. *Take this you evil things.* Then she hesitated. *I might hurt her, I need a different weapon.* The fireball fell from her hand and fizzled to the ground as she devised a new spell. She focused on one winged beastie.

Winged beastie flying round,
Be a frog upon the ground.

She laughed as she watched the flying beastie plunge to the ground to become a bewildered frog. *Getting rid of one at a time is too slow.* A swarm of winged beasties targeted her. *Can I change all of them to frogs? I'm going to try.*

Winged beasties flying toward me,
Now frogs you must be.

The winged beasties instantly became winged frogs. At first, they circled around in a confused pattern, but they quickly reoriented themselves and flew at her. Not wanting to discover what weapons evil winged frogs might have, Maryalise rapidly devised a counterspell.

Winged frogs flying round,
You belong upon the ground.
Wings be gone.

It was not a very good spell. She could not think of a rhyme for gone, but she used the spell anyway. *It works.* She smiled when the frogs plummeted downward. Some landed upright while others landed on their backs, legs jerking in the air.

Maryalise laughed at the confusion of frogs. Her laughter faded as she watched a bindweed vine slither its way behind Aunt Lillian's back to twist itself around Aunt Janet's ankle. She crumpled and fell. Her flashlight flew into the air, smashed to the ground, and winked out. Her arm was twisted at an impossible angle, and she cried out in pain. When she heard her sister's cry, Aunt Lillian rushed to the rescue. She snipped the vine from around Janet's ankle and poured salt upon the pieces. Then she knelt and began to heal the broken arm.

The frogs began to flip over. They bumped into each other because they didn't know how to hop. Their sharp teeth clicked up and down. However, they managed to regroup and resume their attack.

The doubts Maryalise had pushed away before slipped back into her mind. *How long can Thistle keep throwing lightning bolts? The water in the stream and pond are almost gone. How can Denelia continue fighting?* She cried, "Thistle, we are losing. They are so strong, and there are so many of them. Let's open the portal and summon help."

"No," he replied. "We dare not. We fight this battle here and now."

"I know," sighed Maryalise.

She remembered what he had said before. "We must conquer Villiana here. She must never get access to the portal."

The horde of frogs had now formed a circle around her aunts. Each frog had a mouthful of teeth—as sharp as daggers. Their groaning sound was neither a buzz nor a croak, but it hurt Maryalise's ears. The frogs hopped forward and the circle grew smaller. She spoke the first words that came into her mind.

Frogs below me that I see,
Now turned to stone you must be.

The groaning from the frogs abruptly ceased. The teeth didn't snap anymore. Hops were interrupted in midair and they thudded to the ground. Now the frogs were as still as stone. *Because they are stone.* Maryalise smiled. *Take that, you nasty things.*

However, her aunts were still in danger. Shadowy creatures lurched toward them. In that moment, Maryalise forgot that her father had told her to stay by his side. She flew down and landed on the back of a stone frog.

Stone frogs, our protection
I command you to be
Cast an invisible wall
Around my aunts and me.

The horrible creatures snarled as they lurched around the circle of stone frogs, but they could not enter.

The dragon noticed a small flash of light. He saw a tiny fairy fly from the thistle plant to the garden below. He turned his head, and his malevolent eyes blazed a path straight to Maryalise. She felt that evil glare and lifted her head to gaze up into the dragon's fiery eyes. She watched his stomach turn red as he prepared to flame her. The fear she had felt earlier returned and engulfed her. *How do I fight a dragon? I need a dragon to fight this dragon.* She smiled as she remembered a sunset and an almost dragon formed of clouds. Now she called to it.

Almost dragon from far away,
I summon thee here today.

Bring thy fire and thy flame.
Creature of darkness thou must tame.
Almost dragon from far away,
I summon thee, summon thee here this day!

A cloud of white swept into the garden. The misty flame of the almost dragon held all the glowing colors of the sunset. It flew directly toward the dark dragon. The droplets of water in its flame crashed into the fiery flame of the black dragon, turning the flame to steam. The stomach of the black dragon glowed red as the heat increased once more, building up for another flame. The almost dragon flew closer. This time it shot its misty flame at the evil dragon's stomach. The black dragon screamed as it twisted in the sky and took flight. The two dragons vanished into the distance.

Is Villiana gone too? Maryalise looked and saw that the Dark Fairy was hovering in the air where the dragon had been. She stared ominously at Maryalise.

"You miserable pest," snarled Villiana. "I shall rid myself of your meddling magic." She raised one fist.

Maryalise's heart beat faster. She felt powerless to move. *I won't be afraid*, she told herself. *I can't be afraid.* However, the fear in her heart did not go away. She waited helplessly for the Dark Fairy to mutter her incantation, summon her black lightning and cast it down.

Denelia also recognized Villiana's malicious intent and saw her intended target. "No," she cried. "No! Not my child!" She sprang into the air, flying to the rescue. Villiana's black lightning bolt tore through the air, ripped through Denelia's wing, and scorched the flowers just beyond Maryalise.

Denelia spiraled in the air on her uncontrolled descent, and Thistle, arms outstretched, flew to catch her.

"You are losing, Thistle. I am more powerful than you!" Villiana's cruel, triumphant laughter echoed across the dark sky.

How can we win? Maryalise was afraid to look. Her thoughts were jumbled. *Is my mother dead? Villiana is so powerful. How can we possibly win?*

She remembered Thistle's words. "We will fight with truth and light."

With Thistle's words ringing in her mind, Maryalise stood defiantly upon a stone frog. She lifted her arms and called out,

Stars above me in this night.
I summon you and your light.
Though clouds of darkness there may be
Bring your light and come to me.
Trap this darkness with your light.
Make it vanish from our sight.

The sky above her head was a vast expanse of blackness. One star and then another twinkled forth in the darkness. She watched as the stars tumbled from the sky. The darkness was driven back by their light. Maryalise rotated her hands in a circular motion. The stars mimicked the action of her hands, and they became a whirlwind of stars. Stars whirled through the garden. They surrounded the blackness, the remaining winged beasties, the shadowy creatures, the destructive weeds and Villiana. They all were trapped inside that circle of brightness.

Maryalise could no longer see Villiana. The Dark Fairy had disappeared from view inside the darkness that was confined within the circle of light. From out of the darkness, her voice shrieked, "How dare you do this to me? How dare you?"

"Because I can," Maryalise whispered to herself. "I dare because I can."

The whirlwind of stars became smaller and more compact as they imprisoned the dark creatures. All that was inside the circle of stars was forced out of the garden and into the underground cavern. Maryalise listened to their screams of anguished rage. When she could no longer hear their screams, she lowered her hands. Her wings fluttered as her whole body trembled. *I didn't know I could do that. I didn't know it would work.* She smiled as she lowered her hands. *But it did. It did.*

"Thank you, Stars," she said. "Stay and guard that hole."

After the Battle

The garden was silent. The forces of evil had been vanquished. From her perch on the back of a stone frog, Maryalise looked down at Thistle. He stood below her with Denelia's motionless form cradled in his arms. Denelia's face was white and one wing dangled limply. Looking at her father's anguished face, Maryalise cried out, "Is she all right? Is she.—" Maryalise could not finish her question. She wanted to go to her mother, but she could not make herself move.

Aunt Lillian knelt in the grass beside Thistle and held out her hand. "Give her to me. Let me see what I can do." Thistle slowly winged his way upward and tenderly laid his soul mate on Aunt Lillian's outstretched hand.

Fear clutched at Maryalise's heart and squeezed it until she couldn't seem to catch a breath. She felt quivery from her wings to her toes. *Can Aunt Lillian heal Denelia's wing? There is nothing sadder than a grounded fairy*. It was a sad and melancholy fate. She knew that her mother would not be happy if she couldn't fly.

Aunt Lillian cradled Denelia in one hand and gently stroked the damaged wing with the fingertip of the other hand. She murmured soft words. Maryalise could hear the lyrical music of them, but she could not hear the individual words. She was afraid to look, and she was afraid not to look, but she desperately needed to know what was happening. So she looked at Aunt Lillian and watched and worried and hoped. *I'm glad my aunt has healing magic. I'm glad.*

Watching Aunt Lillian heal Denelia's broken wing, Maryalise remembered something her aunt had told her. "When Flora and I decided to stay in the Mortal Dimension, we were allowed to keep a little magic. A mortal's magic is never as strong or as powerful as fairy magic, but a mortal may have some magic. I chose to keep my healing magic."

"And what did Flora choose to keep?" Maryalise had asked, knowing the answer before Aunt Lillian spoke.

"Protecting magic, spells of protection," Aunt Lillian replied.

She looked at her aunts and was glad. *They chose well.* Now she anxiously waited to see what Denelia's fate would be. When her mother lifted her head and smiled, Maryalise felt that she could breathe again.

"Thank you, Thistle," Denelia said. She looked at Maryalise and smiled once more. "I'll be all right," she said.

Aunt Lillian lowered Denelia to the ground, and said, "No flying for a while. You'll need to rest that wing."

Maryalise jumped down from the stone frog to join her parents. She gave Denelia a gentle hug. Thistle smiled approvingly.

"Maryalise, that was a wonderful spell," Thistle said. "You summoned the stars, and they came. A whirlwind of stars. It was beautiful."

"That was powerful magic," Denelia added. "You called the stars and they came."

"They're still here," Maryalise proudly replied. "The stars won't let the darkness out of that hole."

"But they can't stay here forever," Thistle said, "and so we must seal the entrance to the cavern. Our magic will be powerful enough if we all join together."

They stood together and gazed at the twinkling stars dancing around and above the cavern entrance. A feeling of peace and joy and light radiated from the swirling stars and enveloped Maryalise and her family.

In the center of that dancing brightness was the entrance to the cavern. It looked dark and ominous. "Let's close it," Maryalise said. "Let's close it now."

"We will," Denelia replied. "We'll do it now. Let's form a circle of unity around the entrance to the cavern."

Maryalise grinned as they gathered around the cavern entrance. She looked up and up and up at Aunt Janet and Aunt Lillian. Their smiling faces were so very far away. She stretched out her tiny arms as wide as they could reach. "I'm too little," she said. "Denelia and Thistle, you are, too. We'll never manage a circle of unity this way."

Thistle laughed. "We have to be mortal size." The three fairies assumed their mortal size. "We'll need to do this together. The combined words of all of us will make the magic stronger."

Hands were clasped as they made a circle of unity around the entrance to the cavern. The stars seemed to join them in their circle, weaving in and out and dancing above them, enclosing them in a giant sparkling dome.

When the circle was complete, Maryalise formed words in her mind and examined the rhyme and rhythm before she spoke them aloud.

In this garden where flowers sway,
Let them sing their song each day.

Aunt Lillian nodded and smiled as she murmured her words.

Stars that shine with radiant light,
Guard this entrance through the night.

Aunt Janet's words were spoken slowly and surely.

Though evil forces here would come,
Protect us now in this our home.

Denelia softly spoke her words.

> Close this entrance, close it tight.
> Let through no creature of the night.

Then it was Thistle's turn to complete the spell.

> Down below in caverns deep,
> Creatures of evil you must keep.
> Close this entrance, evil's door
> That it may open never more.

The cavern entrance began to shrink. It folded in upon itself until nothing was left except a small depression in the ground and a pile of broken sticks. The bad, prickly feeling was gone. The nasty smell was gone too. Maryalise smiled. She let go of her parents' hands, changed to fairy form and danced with the stars. When she pirouetted in the air, the stars followed her, bestowing their twinkling light on her face, her hands, and her hair.

Her aunts silently watched the magical dance above them. Thistle and Denelia stood with their arms around each other and watched their daughter. Their faces were aglow with love and wonder.

All too soon Denelia said, "Maryalise, it's time to send the stars back to their places."

"But I like them here," she replied as she flew around her parents. She hovered in the air as she explained. "They are so beautiful here in the garden. Let's keep them here for always."

Thistle said, "The sky would be empty and lonely without the stars. Evil would be invisible against the blackness of the sky. You need to let them return home."

"I know." Maryalise brushed away a tear. "I know, but I like having them here. It's all right. You can send them home now."

"I can't do that," said Denelia, "and Thistle can't either. You called them here, and only you can let them go."

"I don't want to," Maryalise repeated. "I like having them here. They are so beautiful." Then she looked into her father's eyes, and she repeated his words. "I know. I can't keep them here. The sky would be empty and lonely without them." She closed her eyes and formed the words in her mind before speaking them.

Stars of beauty, light the night
Return above with thy light.
In sky above, you may play
Until comes the light of day.

A stream of stars circled around Maryalise, twinkled farewell and danced their way heavenward in a blaze of radiant light. She waved good-bye. "Thank you. Thank you. Someday I will come up and dance with you. I promise."

Healing the Garden

Mary Alice stretched her arms above her head. It was morning. She slipped out of bed and went to the window. Leaning on the windowsill, she watched the sun climb over the horizon and shine upon the garden. The sky was awakening and the air was filled with music. She saw a row of brown birds perched on a tree in the garden. They were singing a song of joy and gladness. She waved at them. They bobbed their little heads and continued singing their lilting melody.

Today is my last day in this house and my last day to be Mary Alice. Denelia's wing is healing. Tomorrow Thistle will take Denelia and me through the portal. Mary Alice smiled as she thought about the Fairy Realm. *I'll dance in the meadow and flutter from flower to flower with the butterflies. Thistle will play with me and we'll chase each other through the spray of the waterfall. And maybe I'll fly fast enough to dart between the droplets and not get wet.*

Her cheeks felt wet. She touched a hand to her cheek and realized she was crying. Today was her last day here with Aunt Janet and Aunt Lillian. She wanted to go to the Fairy Realm. She really did, but she didn't want to leave her aunts just yet. *Maybe they could come with us.*

She looked down into the garden and saw that her aunts were talking to her parents who were in their mortal form. I'll ask Thistle, Mary Alice thought as she pulled on her dress. She was too excited to bother with shoes. She ran from her room, hopped onto the banister and slid to the bottom. She laughed as she landed on the floor and ran out the door into the garden. "Thistle, let's take Aunt Janet and Aunt Lillian with us to the Fairy Realm. Can we do that?"

Thistle nodded.

Mary Alice looked at her aunts.

Aunt Janet shook her head back and forth. "And what would I do there? An old mortal woman surrounded by fairies? I chose to be a mortal, and a mortal still I would be."

Aunt Lillian nodded her head. "We would be strangers in that Realm. We would not be fairies. We would still be mortals, without wings, and our feet would be stuck to the ground."

"But then I'll never see you again!" Mary Alice wailed. "I'll miss you. You have to come with us." Her eyes filled with tears again.

"No," Denelia said. "They have the right to choose where they'll live and what they'll be. It's their right." She dried the tears on her daughter's cheeks and said, "I'll miss them too."

Thistle pulled Mary Alice close to him. His other arm reached out to hold Denelia. He looked down into his daughter's eyes. "I know how much you love them. So this is what I will do. I will strengthen the protection spell around this house and garden. This portal will only exist between the garden and the Fairy Realm. All other portals will continue to be locked." Mary Alice smiled as he continued speaking, "And you and your mother will be able to come back and visit whenever you wish."

"And, maybe, Aunt Lillian," Mary Alice exclaimed, "maybe sometimes, when the moon is full, you will come through the portal to see me, and you'll watch me dance with the fairies and the pixies in the meadow."

"Maybe I will, child," Aunt Lillian replied. "Maybe I will."

Mary Alice looked over at her other aunt and said, "And Aunt Janet could come, too."

Aunt Janet smiled and nodded her head. "Maybe," she said.

Mary Alice looked around the garden. It was a scene of devastation. Flowers were broken and trampled. The earth was torn and ravaged. Aunt Lillian began to move through the garden, lifting up bent stems, gathering scattered petals, healing the flowers. Beauty followed in her footsteps as the garden was healed. *Aunt Lillian is healing the garden. I want to help her.*

She helped Aunt Lillian pick up the broken flowers and heal them. When they neared the willow tree, they saw that the stem of the thistle was broken, and its brown leaves lay limply upon the ground. "Oh, no," Mary Alice said.

"We can heal it," her aunt said. "We'll do it together." Mary Alice gently lifted the broken stem, and Aunt Lillian stroked it with light, healing fingers. She touched the leaves, and they became green and fresh. The thistle plant spread out its leaves and lifted itself upright once more. A purple bud formed and spread out its petals to become a full bloom.

Mary Alice's attention was focused on the thistle plant. She was not aware that her father stood beside her until he spoke to the thistle plant. "Grow in safety. Be the guardian of this garden. Watch over it and guard it well."

Aunt Janet was standing beside Thistle. She reached out one finger and touched the thistle blossom. She smiled as she glanced at her sister. "When this thistle goes to seed and sends out its winged messengers, the garden will be full of small thistle plants. Lillian, you will not be pleased."

"Nay," said Thistle. "The garden shall not be filled with thistles. I'll cast a spell on this plant. Its seeds shall fly and plant themselves along the borders of this garden. They shall be invisible to all mortal eyes, but they will encircle this garden. Evil shall not enter here." Aunt Lillian smiled and nodded her approval.

Denelia sat on the porch swing and watched the garden return to life. She smiled and waved as she swung back and forth. Thistle, Aunt Janet, and Aunt Lillian walked through the garden to join Denelia on the porch, but Mary Alice remained in the garden. She wandered down one path and up another. The garden was filled with blossoms of every color. She crawled into her secret place. The magic protecting spell was still there. The circle of rocks had kept evil out. She sat cross-legged, enjoying the magical feeling in the shelter of the willow tree. However, there was so much joy in her heart that she could not sit still. She parted the willows and scrambled out. She became Maryalise and flew from flower to flower.

A feeling of contentment enveloped her and vibrated through her whole being. She hovered above the thistle plant and listened to the song of the flowers. The garden had been healed. She expected a symphony of sight and sound to greet her. As the melody drifted through the air and into her heart, she frowned. It didn't sound quite right. There were wrong notes and missing notes. While she pondered this new puzzle, she saw a small brown rabbit sitting motionless near the path. *He looks sad. He looks really sad.*

She looked at the rabbit and remembered flying up through his hole with Thistle. *Oh no. The rabbit hole. It connects the cavern and the garden. If the flying beasties find it, they can come back to the garden. It must be sealed.*

She began devising a spell to seal this last opening to the cavern below. The ray of sunlight had returned with the dawn and was sentinel here once more, but she knew it could not stay forever to guard this hole. When night came, it would have to leave. She looked into the rabbit's sad eyes again. "I know. It is your home. You don't want that hole in the bottom." She took a deep breath, gathered her thoughts and said.

This small hole is rabbit's home.
Through it let no evil come.

She picked up a tiny pebble, flew into the air and threw the pebble down the hole.

> Let this rock that down I throw
> Roll to the end and grow and grow.
> Block that entrance—block it tight.
> Make it strong against evil's might.
> This small hole is rabbit's home.
> Through it let no evil come.

Maryalise thought that she saw the rabbit smile and she smiled, too. She could feel the music in the garden surround her once more. Now the healing of the garden was complete. She looked and listened. The song of the flowers filled the garden. It was a symphony of sight and sound.

Maryalise whispered to herself, "I hear the flowers singing."

Maryalise and the Stolen Years Preview Invitation

You are invited to preview Maryalise and the Stolen Years which will be published in the summer of 2019.

Maryalise and the Stolen Years

A dragon rose from the horizon, trailing darkness in its wake. Each beat of his wings brought fierce winds howling across the sky. Churning and twisting blackness swallowed up the blue sky as the dragon swept toward Maryalise.

Fluttering her wings rapidly, the tiny fairy struggled to remain in place as the dragon's powerful wings carried him closer. Strands of honey brown hair whipped across Maryalise's face, and her pink tunic twisted around her knees. The young fairy stared, drawn by a mysterious force. "I feel magic," she muttered. "Evil magic." When the dragon came closer

Maryalise saw the silhouette of a fairy—mortal size, wings outstretched—standing on the dragon's back. The fairy's purple dress swirled behind her in the wind. When Maryalise tried to see the fairy's face, she felt a force seek entrance into her mind.

It's not the dragon who controls this magic, thought Maryalise, *it's the fairy who rides upon his back.*

The dragon and the fairy continued to advance. Now Maryalise could see the fairy's face.

"Villiana?" Maryalise whispered. "Can it be?"

She shook her head in disbelief. *I know Villiana rides a dark dragon. But we used strong magic. We sealed her into an underground cavern. She can't hurt me.* Even as she thought those words, a niggling twinge of fear oozed into her heart.

The forward motion of the dragon stopped abruptly, and he hovered in front of the dainty fairy. She gazed into the eyes of the Dark Fairy. "Villiana," Maryalise whispered and her wings fluttered faster. *It is Villiana. What does she want now?*

Villiana raised her fists, sending coils of darkness curling outward. Maryalise was unable to move. The evil cocoon surrounded Maryalise, Villiana, and the dragon.

The wind howled, the dark smoke twisted and a soft, compelling voice called, "Maryalise, Maryalise, listen to me."

Maryalise covered her ears with her hands. But she still heard Villiana call to her.

No, thought Maryalise. *No. I will not listen. I will not listen.*

The words of the Dark Fairy name came into her mind—even though they were not spoken aloud.

"Maryalise, you must listen to me," the mind-voice said.

Maryalise slid her eyes away from the fairy's gaze and stared down at her feet. "I will not look at her," she chanted to herself. "I will not listen to her." The mind-voice of the Dark Fairy faded as Maryalise repeated these words over and over and over. She stared intently at her toes. *What is Villiana doing? What evil magic is she using now*? She chanced a quick glance upward, and her gaze locked with that of the Dark Fairy.

The mind-voice grew louder, more insistent. "Maryalise. Maryalise. Look at me. Keep looking at me. You must listen to me."

She's winning. I can't stop looking at her. I can't stop hearing her. Maryalise balled her fists at her side. *I must keep fighting. But she's so beautiful.* A silver crown set with black gems circled the Dark Fairy's head, resting on glossy black hair. Her purple dress was gossamer thin—as if it had been woven by spiders.

Villiana smiled and stretched her arms out toward the tiny fairy. The Dark Fairy spoke aloud with a soft melodious voice. "I have found you, my child. Come to me. Come to me." Maryalise fluttered her wings and began to move toward Villiana.

"Yes," Villiana crooned. "Yes. Come to me, my child. You will be a princess in a magical dimension. We will be together again."

"I remember those words. I've heard them before," murmured Maryalise. For a moment she thought, *Yes, this beautiful fairy has come to claim me.* Maryalise moved a little closer to the Dark Fairy. *A princess. I'm a princess.*

Maryalise's captive mind welcomed the Dark Fairy's words, but her reluctant heart held back. She hesitated.

Villiana did not notice the young fairy hesitate. "You are a princess. You are my princess." The Dark Fairy smiled triumphantly. *Thistle*, she thought, *I have won. Today I claim your child.*

Maryalise's ears heard the fairy's words, but her mind heard Villiana's thoughts. "Thistle,"Maryalise murmured. "Thistle is my father. Thistle loves me." The connection between Villiana and Maryalise faltered. *My father won't let her have me.*

Villiana continued to summon her. "Come to me, my child. Come." Maryalise no longer wished to be connected, but the coils of smoke twisted around her and drew her forward.

"Thistle! Where are you?" Maryalise tried to see him through the darkness that surrounded her. She called to her mother. "Denelia! Help me!" But there was no answer. *They're gone. My parents left without me. I was invisible when I followed them through the portal, and they didn't see me. They don't know that I'm here.*

The circle of darkness tightened. *This smoke is like a wall, and I'm trapped.* Despair snaked its way into her heart. She heard a hiss. Something hard touched her skin. Something snapped at her wrist.

"No!" she cried, "No!" She twisted her arm, focused her magic and tried to block that hard, cold thing.

> I summon magic now,
> Magic inside me,
> Make this. . . this. . . this . . .

Maryalise couldn't name that something that snapped at her arm. She couldn't find words for the rest of her spell. She felt the snap again, and she was afraid that it was too late. She cried,

> With all the power inside me,
> I summon magic to set me free.
> Hear this call and hear it well.
> Free me from this evil spell.

Sparkles glistened inside the darkness. *Good.* Maryalise watched a small thread of brightness pierce the dark cloud. The sparkles of her spell united with it. She grasped that thread of magic and slipped free.

She heard Villiana's furious scream. "Maryalise, return to me. You are mine! You will be mine!" Villiana's voice faded in the distance, and then it was gone.

The thread of magic vanished. Silence enveloped Maryalise. Her wings quivered and her hands trembled. She waited for the wildness of her heart to subside.

When she looked around, she saw that she was standing on a soft green something. Green hung above her head. Green hung before her eyes. *Where am I?* She reached out and touched a green leaf—a prickly green leaf. *This is a thistle plant*, she realized. *I've landed on a thistle plant. I feel safe.*

"It was Villiana," she whispered to herself. "How did she escape from that underground cavern? And why does she want me?" Her heart resumed its rapid beat, but she willed herself to be calm.

Did she follow me here? Does she know where I am? Maryalise listened with her ears, her heart, and her magic. She slowly pushed the thistle leaves aside and peeked out. She was alone.

She flew between the leaves and into the air. Her thistle plant was growing next to a small, weathered tombstone. *This is a graveyard. I'm in a cemetery*. It was an old one, a forgotten cemetery. The ancient graves were neglected. Some stones leaned precariously while others lay broken upon the ground. It was evident that no one came to remember, to mourn, or to honor those who were buried here. Small thistles grew, scattered among the graves.

Maryalise flew to a tall tombstone and sat down. She folded her wings and drew her knees up to her chin. *How did I get here? Someone rescued me? Who? And why?* She asked the questions, but she couldn't think of any answers. *Maybe Thistle and Denelia will know*.

"I guess it's time to go home, even if they get mad at me—even if I did get myself into this mess. All I wanted," sighed Maryalise, "was to help my parents look for Pansy and Willow."

Earlier that day she had heard Thistle and Denelia, her parents, talking. They were planning to leave her in the Fairy Realm while they traveled to other dimensions to search for two fairy children that Villiana had stolen. She remembered thinking, *Who do they think I am? A baby? I'm twelve. I have powerful magic. I want to go with them, but if I ask to go with them, they will tell me I can't. So I won't ask.*

After her parents had hugged her and said goodbye, Maryalise had made herself invisible. She had followed her parents through the portal. She was an invisible shadow that they didn't see or sense. Then the dragon came. Attention riveted on the dragon, she had not noticed when her parents left.

Her thoughts returned to the present. No longer feeling quite so safe, she decided, *I guess it's time to go home. I need to tell my parents that Villiana has escaped from the cavern. After they scold me, maybe we can discover what Villiana wants now.*

She stood up, closed her eyes, and chanted her spell.

I am Maryalise.
Maryalise is me.
The Fairy Realm
Is where I want to be.

She did not feel the tingle that usually accompanied her spells. A cold empty feeling seemed to gather around her and she opened her eyes. She was still in the cemetery. Maryalise took a deep breath and repeated her spell.

Nothing happened.

The words of her spell sparkled and then vanished. They seemed to be attracted to the curious metal bracelet on her arm. It had a snake with two heads and the body of the snake was coiled around her wrist. Maryalise carefully examined it. There was a hinge on one side. The edges didn't seem to line up correctly. One edge hung below the bottom edge of the other—like a shirt with the buttons in the wrong holes. She pulled on the mismatched edges, but the bracelet would not open. The metal felt cold, and she sensed evil.

Maryalise's fingers trembled. The trembling crept inside her. It coiled deeper and wrapped itself around her heart. "This must be Villiana's doing," she muttered, and her fear became indignation. "She shall not win! Thistle will not let her."

She took a deep breath, thought of her parents, and voiced her spell.

Thistle, Denelia, hear my plea,
Please come. Rescue me.

She watched as one of the snake heads rose up from the bracelet and hissed. The other snake head swallowed the words of her spell.

Maryalise and the Stolen Years available Summer 2019

Acknowledgements

So many of my friends and family have believed in me and supported me on this fantastic journey from story idea to publication. The idea for Maryalise and the Singing Flowers began in a creative writing class as a response to a prompt. After three weeks of writing about this girl, I realized that she had a story I wanted to share.

I appreciate my family and friends who have patiently read and critiqued my writing. Thank you to my many beta readers who had good ideas and suggestions. I wish to especially thank my daughter Linda who was not afraid to rip into my book and point out my inconsistencies and suggest ways to improve this story.

About the Author

Rose Owens is a professional storyteller and has shared stories for over 40 years. She enjoys telling traditional folktales, multicultural stories, family stories and her own original stories. She says that storytelling is like spinning a silver web that invites listeners to come and be part of the storytelling experience. Her listeners are always mesmerized by her oral storytelling skills. The Maryalise trilogy, born in her imagination and recorded on paper, is an invitation to enter a make-believe world.

Originally from Utah, Rose now lives in California. She graduated from Brigham Young University with a degree in education. She and her husband have seven children, twenty-one grandchildren and 2 great-grand-daughters—all of whom enjoy hearing her stories. She enjoys writing, art, reading, and traveling to see her family.

Books by Rose Owens

Who Was There: A Nativity Story for Children
https://www.amazon.com/s?url=search-alias%3Daps&field-keywords=Who+Was+There+Rose+Owens

Maryalise Trilogy:

- Maryalise and the Singing Flowers
- Maryalise and the Stolen Years – available Summer 2019
- Maryalise and the Snatched Fairy - available Fall 2019

http://www.Rosethestorylady.net
email address: rosethestorylady@gmail.com

Before you leave:

- Please write a review
- Visit http://www.rosethestorylady.net to see bonus material. Find out how Maryalise had her beginnings. Read deleted material and content that never made it into the book. Spoiler alert: It is recommended that you read all of *Maryalise and the Singing Flowers* before looking at the bonus material.

Made in the USA
Middletown, DE
20 February 2020